Chapter 1 自我介紹的開端

被要求做自我介紹
自己主動做自我介紹
介紹朋友給他人
帶朋友一同參加活動
表達已經見過面了
表明自己是誰介紹的
請人幫忙引見自己

Chapter 2 打破僵局

問好
以問候語開場
初見面的客氣話
找尋共同點
主動介紹自己
與對方相關的話題
讚美對方
引導對方發表意見或評論
搭訕

Chapter 3 談個性秉性

形容性格優缺點的常用語
聰明，精明，警覺，反應快

My Self-Introduction in English

最簡單的
英文自我介紹

讓我們用最簡單的句子
幫助您完成一篇最漂亮的自我介紹吧

U0074453

陳久娟★編著

序

　　無論多少人認為「第一印象」可以在彼此熟識之

不可諱言的，好的第一印象絕對可以為您的人際關係

人給人的印象好壞，除儀態之外，就是談吐了。

　　第一次見面，以自我介紹為開端的機會不勝枚舉

化的時代，深愛旅遊的你，經常出差的你，喜歡夜生

網際網路的你，甚至是著迷於線上遊戲的你，是否經

紹自己？卻往往在介紹完名字後，腦中便一片空白，

些什麼…總懊惱著，可以漂亮地展現自己多好，真可

點點。

　　即使只要花十五秒便能聽完或讀完的自傳或是自

扮演的角色，便是在這關鍵的十五秒內成功地推銷自

象深刻。千萬別小看這十五秒喔，在事事求表現的現

延伸自己停留在對方腦海裡的時間，都算是一次成功

　　本書即將帶給您的驚喜，不是準備一堆範例要您

時之需。而是將一篇篇自我介紹化整為零，以最簡單

如此一來，不管您需要的是兩三句話就搞定的自我介

令教授或主管印像深刻的自傳，順著章節找出適合您

很快的，一篇獨一無二的自我介紹，就漂亮地完成

耐心，穩定，鎮定

好奇，有創意，有天份

仁慈，寬容，同情

友善，熱情

外向，獨立，樂觀

謙恭，溫和，體貼，耐心，有禮

保守，謹慎

安靜，內向

真誠，大方，可信賴，坦率

愉悅，樂觀，幽默

公正無私，正派

有能力，有效率

節儉，勤奮，認真

積極，強勢

Chapter 4 談個人基本資料

個人資料

星座

生肖

血型

生長背景，居住環境

婚姻狀況

家庭狀況

基本健康狀況

外表及文化背景

Chapter 5 談學習經歷

修習課程

修習學位

求學過程

學業成績

專業考試

學歷

概談曾受過的教育

Chapter 6 談工作經歷

最簡單的職業類別自我介紹

工作經歷

工作職掌

工作時間

工作地點

部門及職稱

曾參與的重要事務、工作成就或外派出差

所從事的行業類別

薪資及福利

職位上應具有的特點為何

什麼經驗都沒有的話怎麼辦

Contents

Chapter 7 談人生經歷及生涯規畫

人生的轉折點
家庭經歷
出國經歷
克服失敗獲得成功的經歷
從參與的活動中啟發感想
未來發展方向及生涯規劃
表達信念及看法
常用的鼓勵式短語

Chapter 8 專長及嗜好

嗜好
沒有嗜好
特殊專長
社團
語言能力評鑑

Chapter 9 結語

道別語
道謝
臨別時的客套語

最簡單的英文自我介紹

Chapter 10 簡短自我介紹

商務環境自我介紹
對新朋友自我介紹
履歷表封面的簡單介紹

Chapter 11 一分鐘寫自傳

自傳的基本架構
自傳常用單字分類

Chapter 12 談話的藝術

不該談的話題
絕對安全的話題
個人資料表重點資訊（中英對照）

· Chapter 1 ·

自我介紹的開端
Starting A Self Introduction

★被要求做自我介紹

Tell me about yourself.
Talk about yourself!
Tell me something about yourself.
Describe yourself, please.
請介紹一下你自己吧。
談一談你自己吧！
請描述一下你自己。

Introduce yourself briefly, please.
請介紹一下你自己。

What can you tell me about yourself?
請説説自己是怎樣的人？

Why don't you tell me a little about yourself?
何不稍微介紹一下你自己？

How would your friends describe you?
你的朋友都怎麼形容你？

How would you describe yourself?
你認為自己是怎樣的人？

記憶關鍵：	
briefly	簡短的
describe	描述

★自己主動做自我介紹

Let me introduce myself.
讓我自我介紹一下。

Please allow me to introduce myself.
請允許我做個自我介紹。

May I introduce myself?
我可以自我介紹一下嗎？

Do you mind if I introduce myself?
不介意我自我介紹一下吧？

Let me do some introduction about myself.
讓我來介紹一下自己。

It's my great honor to introduce myself to you here.
It's my pleasure to introduce myself to you here.
I'm very happy to introduce myself to you.
很榮幸在這兒向大家做自我介紹。

What do you want to know about myself?
您想知道我哪方面的情況呢？

Let's get to know each other.
讓我們了解一下彼此吧。

記憶關鍵：

introduction	介紹（名詞）
It's my honor/pleasure to...	我很榮幸…
Please allow me to...	請容我…

★介紹朋友給他人

Hey, Larry! Meet John!
嗨，Larry！見過 John！（非正式的用法）

Larry, I want you to meet John
Larry，我想為你引見 John。

Larry, this is John!
Larry，這是 John！

Allow me to introduce my friend, John, to you.
請允許我向你介紹我的朋友 John。

May I present Mr. John White（to you）?
請允許我（向您）介紹 John White 先生。（正式的用法）

May I introduce Mr. John White?
讓我來介紹一下 John White 先生。

Can I propose my friend, John, for this job?
我可以介紹 John 擔任這項工作?

Would you like to meet my friend, John?
請容我介紹我的朋友，John？

記憶關鍵：

meet sb.	見過某人
introduce	介紹（動詞）
present, propose	呈現，或在公開場合引見

最簡單的英文自我介紹

★帶朋友一同參加活動

May I bring my friends, John, to the party with me?
我可以帶我的朋友 John 一起來參加這個派對嗎?

May I bring a friend?
我可以帶個朋友來嗎?

May I bring my friend along?
可以帶朋友來嗎?

Can I take a friend?
我可以帶朋友來嗎?

What if I bring a friend of mine?
如果我帶一個朋友去呢?

I am bringing a friend of mine from work.
我會帶一個工作上的朋友來。

I will invite a special guest.
我會邀請一位神秘嘉賓來。

I will ask someone to join with me.
I will request someone to come with me.
我會請一個人跟我一起來。

記憶關鍵：

ask, request	請求
invite	邀請
bring, take	帶（人或物）
special guest	神秘嘉賓

★表達已經見過面了

We've met!
我們見過面了！

We've met before!
我們見過面了！

We've met each other.
我們彼此見過了。

We are familiar with each other.
我們很熟。

We go way back!
我們認識很久了。（較口語的說法）

We have known each other for a long time.
我們認識很久了。（一般的說法）

I am acquainted with John.
我已經認識 John 了。

I know John very well.
我跟 John 很熟。

I know the face.
看起來很眼熟。
（見過對方的臉，但臨時叫不出名字的狀況。）

記憶關鍵：	
familiar	熟悉

★表明自己是誰介紹的

It's James who introduced me to Mr. Woods.
是 James 介紹我給 Mr. Woods 的。

I am a friend of Johnson's from his work.
我是 Johnson 工作上的朋友。

I am Johnson's work associate.
我是 Johnson 的同事。

I am Johnson's high school buddy.
我是 Johnson 的高中死黨。

I am a friend of Johnson's.
我是 Johnson 的朋友。

I am here with Johnson.
I came with Johnson.
我跟 Johnson 一起來的。

Johnson referred me here.
Johnson 介紹我來的。

Johnson introduced me here.
Johnson 介紹我來這裡的。

記憶關鍵：

refer	介紹
referral	介紹人
from sb's work	某人工作上（認識的朋友）。

★請人幫忙引見自己

Can you fix me up with James?
你幫我介紹 James 好嗎？（尤其用在介紹約會對象）

Can you fix up a date for me?
你幫我介紹一個約會對象吧？（用在介紹約會對象）

Could you introduce me to the manager?
你能為我引見經理嗎？

Would you arrange a meeting for us, please?
你可以為我們安排會面嗎？

Would you please introduce me to the lady over there?
你可以幫我介紹一下那邊那位小姐嗎？

Would you send this （drink） to the lady over there?
麻煩你把這杯（飲料）送過去給那位小姐？
（在酒吧向人搭訕的伎倆之一。）

You are the member, can you bring me in the club?
你已經是會員了，可以介紹我進那個俱樂部嗎？

Can you bring me in?
你可以帶（介紹）我進去（某場合）嗎？

記憶關鍵：

arrange	安排
introduce A to B	將 A 介紹給 B
bring sb in	將某人帶入某場合

·Chapter 2·

打破僵局
Break the Ice

★問好

Hello!
Hi!
大家好！

Hi, there.
Hello, everyone.
嗨，各位。
（較隨興的打招呼方式）

What's up?
最近好嗎？

How are you?
你好嗎？

How do you do.
你好。

How's your day?
今天過的如何？

How's everything?
Is everything ok?
一切都還好嗎？

★以問候語開場

Good morning!
早安!

Good day!
日安!

Good afternoon!
午安!

Good evening!
晚安!
你(們)好!

How are you?
你好嗎?
你們好嗎?

記憶關鍵:

Good evening 及 Good night 的使用時機不同。Evening 泛指傍晚到晚上的時間,比如在晚宴中向賓客問好時,便是說good evening。至於 Good night 則有道別的意義,比如:在睡前道晚安,或是晚宴結束送客道別。

★初見面的客氣話

I've heard a lot about you.
久仰大名。

Hello, nice to meet you.
Very nice to meet you.
Glad to meet you.
Great to meet you.
Pleased to meet you.
很高興見到你。
（限用於初次見面的朋友。）

Nice to see you again.
Glad to see you again.
Pleased to see you again.
Great to meet you again.
很高興見到你。
（限用於曾見過面但不太熟的朋友。）

How have you been?
一切都還好嗎？
（同樣限用於曾見過面但不太熟的朋友。）

記憶關鍵：	
hear about	聽說，得知
again	再次
nice to...	很高興，很榮幸
glad to...	很高興，很榮幸
great to...	很高興，很榮幸
pleased to...	很高興，很榮幸

★找尋共同點

How do you know about this trip?
你怎麼知道有這個旅遊資訊？
（Trip 可用各種「事件或資訊」置換。）

How do you know James?
你怎麼認識 James 的？

Are you a friend of Johnson, too?
你也是 Johnson 的朋友啊？

You also like fashion show, right?
你也喜歡看時尚秀，是吧？

What brings you here?
What brings you in?
Why are you here?
Why are you in?
你怎麼會來呢？
什麼風把你吹來的？（雙方碰巧在同一場合出現時。）

What brings you here on a night like this?
你怎麼會來參加這個晚宴呢？（只要是晚上的時間見到面，都可以這麼說）

Do you like the party?
你喜歡這個派對嗎？

Do you come here often, too?
你也常來這裡嗎？

★ 主動介紹自己

I am Lucy.
我叫 Lucy。

Lucy.
我是 Lucy。
（一邊說一邊伸手與對方握手，或是舉酒杯向對方致意等。）

Hi, I am Johnson. I am a friend of the hostess.
嗨，我是 Johnson。我是女主人的朋友。

I am here with my friend.
我跟朋友一起來的。

Hi, my name is Rose, a friend of the bride.
嗨，我是 Rose，我是新娘的朋友。

I am Rose. I am with the groom.
我是 Rose。我是新郎的親友。

I am with the groom's party.
I am with the bride's party.
我是新郎的朋友。
我是新娘的朋友。

I am George. John's old friend, we go way back.
我是 George，John 的老朋友。我們認識很久了。

★與對方相關的話題

Are you here with your family?
你跟家人一起來的嗎？

Are you here for a business trip?
Are you here on a business trip?
你是來這裡出差的嗎？

Are you here for the trade show?
你也來參展嗎？

Where are you from?
Where are you from originally?
你是哪裡人？

What do you do?
What do you do for living?
你的工作是什麼？

Just arrive?
（你也是）剛到嗎？

When did you arrive?
你什麼時候到的？

記憶關鍵：

for a business trip 或是 on a business 意義上只有些許差距，
一般是可以通用的。
for 有「因為」的意思。Are you here FOR XXX? 你是「為」
了 XXX 而來的嗎？

★讚美對方

Way to go!
Nice job.
Good for you!
Not bad!
幹得好。/ 好極了！/ 不賴嘛！

I am impressed.
我（對你）印象深刻。

What a lovely place!
真是一個好地方啊！

You're on top of it!
You are great!
你真厲害！

You look great today.
你今天看起來精神不錯。（也可用來形容穿著不錯）

Nice outfit!
你的衣服真好看！（outfit 泛指所有的外衣）

What is it made of?
What is it made out of?
這是什麼質料？

Is this the latest Spring collection?
這是今春最新款嗎？

★引導對方發表意見或評論

Great movie, isn't it?
電影滿好看的，你覺得呢？（電影發表會上）

The movie sucks, right?
電影真難看，對吧？

Nice dissert, right?
甜點還不錯，對吧？（茶會或聚餐場合）

Isn't it nice?
真是不錯吧？

Do you enjoy the show?
你喜歡這個表演嗎？

How do you think about the movie?
你覺得這部電影如何？

How do you feel about the ending?
你覺得這部電影的結局如何？

Which designer do you prefer?
你喜歡哪個設計師？（在時尚發表會上）

What would you do if it were you?
如果是你，你會怎麼做？

記憶關鍵：

「誘導」對方說出自己的看法，進而引發一段討論。

★搭訕

Excuse me, my name is Sam.
打擾一下，我的名字叫做 Sam。

Have we met?
我們見過面嗎？

Do we know each other?
我們認識嗎？

Are you Tina? I am Steven.
你是 Tina 嗎?我是 Steven。

Are you here with someone else?
你跟誰一起來的？

Are you along?
你一個人嗎？

Has the seat taken?
這個位置有人坐嗎？

Can I join you?
我可以跟你一起坐嗎？

Can we make friends?
我們可以做朋友嗎？

Lovely day, isn't it?
天氣真好，對不對？

記憶關鍵：

禮貌性的拒絕搭訕，可以這麼說：

I am sorry, the seat is taken.
抱歉，這個位置有人坐了。

I am here with someone else.
我跟朋友一起來。

I am not along.
我不是一個人。（朋友在附近的意思。）

I am expecting someone else.
我在等人。

I believe not.
我想不認識吧。（拒絕搭訕式地問題 Have we met? 時）

I don't think we've seen each other before.
我想我們不認識吧！

I think this isn't a good idea.
我想這並不是一個好主意。

• Chapter 3 •

談個性秉性
Personality

★形容性格優缺點的常用語

I am a good person.
I am a nice person.
I am kind.
I am a kind person.
我是一個好人。
我心地很好。

I am an easy going person.
我個性隨和。

I am pretty reliable.
我很可靠。

I think I am sincere and honest.
我想我是一個真切而誠實的人。

I am a considerate person.
I am very considerate.
我是一個深思熟慮的人。
我對任何事情都考慮周到。

I tend to be considerate and civilizing
我比較細心又有教養。

I am a rational person.
I am pretty rational.
我是一個理性的人。

I am pretty open-minded.
我心胸很開放，沒有偏見。

I usually offer refinement in my interaction with people and animals.
不管對人或對動物,我總是以優雅的態度與他們互動。

I have a charming personality.
我的個性很迷人。

記憶關鍵:

charming 也可以用來形容長相迷人,很有魅力的意思。

I always persist till the end.
我總是堅持到最後。

I am firm and persistent.
我的性格堅毅。

I used to gives people a very good first impression.
我總是給人很好的第一印象。

記憶關鍵:

first impression = first image 第一印象

I have clean definition for people or things.
我對人對事都是好惡分明。

I am a good listener.
我是一個很好的傾聽者。

I am a romantic person.
I am romantic.
我是一個浪漫的人。

Sometimes I am a little bit defensive.
有時候我有點防禦心。

I am very sensitive.
我很敏感。
我很敏銳。

I have high self-esteem.
我自尊心很強。

記憶關鍵：

相反詞就是 low self-esteem.（沒有自尊心）。

I am tolerant of different views.
我可以容忍許多不同的意見。

I am quite sentimental sometimes.
我有時多愁善感。

I am picky.
我很挑剔。

Some people said I love to show off.
有些人說我很愛現。

I always find opportunities to show off my strength.
我總是找機會表現自己的優點。

Sometime I am unpredictable.
有時候我滿出乎人預料的。

I am confident.
我有自信。

最簡單的英文自我介紹

I have confidence in myself.
我對自己有信心。

Some people think I am mysterious, but I am not.
有些人覺得我很神秘,其實不然。

I am a righteous man.
I have a strong sense of justice.
我是一個有正義感的人。
我有很強烈的正義感。

I am generous.
我很慷慨。

I have stable character.
我性格很穩定。

I am a perfectionist.
我是一個完美主義者。

I am a brave girl.
我是個勇敢的女孩。

相反性格的形容詞

stubborn	頑固

★聰明，精明，警覺，反應快

I am smart.
I am clever.
I am intelligent.
我滿聰明的。

I am witty.
我很機智。

I am always on the alert.
I always remain watchful.
我警覺性很高。

I am very sensible.
我很明智。

I am a witty person.
我是一個機智的人。
我是一個説話風趣的人。

I am quit sharp-minded.
我很富機智。

I am fun loving.
我是一個風趣的人。

I am a shrewd business man.
我是一個精明的生意人。

People describe me as an ingenious person.
我朋友常説我是一個足智多謀的人。

I am quick.
我反應很快。

I am a quick learner.
我學得很快。

I am a quick thinker.
我是一個反應靈敏的人。

I am always energetic.
我永遠精力充沛。

I am pretty active.
我很積極。
我很活潑。

相反性格的形容詞

ignorant	無知的
clumsy	笨拙的
stupid	愚笨的
silly	愚笨的
awkward	尷尬的，笨拙的

★耐心，穩定，鎮定

I am always patient.
我總是很有耐心。

I have a lot of patience.
我很有耐心。

I am patient, persevering, conscientious, sensitive and self-controlled.
我很有耐心，堅忍，認真，敏銳且有自制力。

I am pretty calm under stress.
我面對壓力很鎮定。

相反性格的形容詞

depressed	壓抑的
uneasy	焦慮不安的
dependent	依賴的
fragile	脆弱的，易碎的
unstable	不穩定
paranoid	偏執的，神經質的
agitated	焦慮

★好奇，有創意，有天份

I am very creative.
I have a lot of creativity.
我很有創意。

I am imaginative.
我很有想像力。

I have a lot of creative ideas to inspire my next project.
我有許多有創意的點子作為我下一個專案的靈感。

I am always curious about new technologies.
我對於新科技總是感到好奇。

I am pretty talented.
我滿有天份的。

I have talent for playing piano.
我對彈鋼琴有天份。

I am versatile and talented.
我很多才多藝又有天份。

★仁慈，寬容，同情

I am kind.
I am a kind-hearted man.
我心地很善良。

I am a caring person.
I am very caring.
我是一個有愛心的人。

I'm not particularly wealthy, but I am charitable.
我並不特別富有，但我很慷慨（慈悲）。

I am actually quite benevolent and compassionate.
事實上，我滿有愛心也滿有同情心的。

I always have great compassion for patients.
我對病人總是很有同情心。

I am humane.
我很仁慈。

I am merciful and generous.
我是仁慈且大方的。

I am really sympathetic for that little girl.
我對那位小女孩感到很同情。

I am compassionate.
我很有同情心。

★友善，熱情

I am a very social person.
I am very sociable.
我很合群。
我很愛交際。

I am very hospitable and approachable.
我很殷勤，很容易接近。

I am friendly.
我很友善。

The family is very nice and warmhearted.
這個家庭非常友善且熱心。

I can find many warmhearted people in this community.
你在這裡可以認識許多熱心的人。

I am a warmhearted and easy to approach person.
我是一個熱心且很有親和力的人。

I am enthusiastic about movie business.
I have passion for movie business.
我對電影有熱情。

I am kind and enthusiastic.
我有愛心且熱忱。

I am passionate.
我很熱情。

★外向，獨立，樂觀

I have a pleasant and optimistic character.
我的性格開朗樂觀。

I am quite sociable.
我很善交際。

I am an extrovert person.
我是一個外向的人。

I am independent.
我很獨立。

My parents trained me to be really independent.
我父母親把我訓練成非常獨立的個性。

I have optimistic by nature.
我天性樂觀。

相反性格的形容詞

eccentric	古怪的
odd	古怪的，奇怪的
strange	奇怪的
pessimistic	悲觀的
introverted	內向，不愛交際
timid	膽小

★謙恭，溫和，體貼，耐心，有禮

I've grown up to be a kind, mild, outgoing person.
我已經長成了一個仁慈，溫和，外向的人。

I am a humble person.
我是一個謙恭的人。

I am courteous to everyone.
我對每個人都很有禮貌。

I am a thoughtful person.
我是一個體貼的人。

I am a mild-mannered person.
I have a mild-temper
我是一個溫和的人。

相反性格的形容詞

scornful	輕蔑的，蔑視的
superficial	膚淺的
shallow	膚淺的
showy	炫耀的
pretentious	矯飾的
extravagant	奢侈的
conceited	驕傲的，自負的
hypocrisy	虛偽的
insincere	不真誠的
dishonest	不誠實的
deceitful	欺詐的，不老實的
hypocritical	虛偽的

★保守，謹慎

I am conservative.
我個性保守。

I am very reserved.
我很拘謹。

I am a conservative person.
我是一個個性保守的人。

Asian women tend to be more reserved.
亞洲女性觀念比較保守一點。

I am willing to obey the manager's instructions.
我願意服從經理的指示。

I tend to be obedient to rules.
我比較喜歡遵守規定。

I am careful to details.
我對細節很重視。
我對細節很小心

I am cautious about making promise.
我對承諾很謹慎。

相反性格的形容詞

ill-advised	輕率的，不明智的
unintentional	無意的
impulsive	衝動的，莽撞的

rude	魯莽的
hasty	倉促的，草率的
careless	粗心大意的
thoughtless	粗心大意的
half-hearted	不認真的
neglectful	疏忽的
offensive	討厭的，無禮的
reckless	不計後果的
daring	大膽的
bold	大膽的

★安靜，內向

I'm an introvert person.
我是一個內向的人。

I am a shy person.
我是一個害羞的人。

I am kind of quiet.
我個性有點文靜。

I am silent.
I am a quiet person.
我很安靜。

★真誠，大方，可信賴，坦率

I am pretty reliable.
我很可靠。

I am generous to everybody.
我對所有人都很寬宏大量。

I am generous in giving help to others.
我對其他人總是慷慨提供協助。

I am a straightforward person.
我是一個正直的人。
我是一個直接而坦率的人。

I am frank and genuine.
我個性直率真誠。

記憶關鍵：

to be frank with you….	我老實跟你說吧…
to be honest with you…	我老實跟你說吧…
frankly speaking,…	老實說…
honestly….	老實說…
frankly…	老實說…

I am earnest in my works.
我對工作的態度很認真。

I am an honest and sincere person.
我是一個誠實且認真的人。

I am a very responsible and reliable person.
我是一個很負責任，可依賴的人。

I am an experienced and trustworthy guide.
我是一個很有經驗，很值得信任的導遊。

I am dependable.
我是一個可信賴的人。

相反性格的形容詞

suspicious	多疑的
self-assertive	自作主張的
ingenuous	天真無邪的
naive	天真的，幼稚的

★愉悅，樂觀，幽默

I have a cheerful and optimistic personality.
我擁有令人愉快且樂觀的性格。

I have sense of humor.
我有幽默感。

I am creative and humorous.
我很有創意且很有幽默感。

相反性格的形容詞

pessimistic	悲觀
reluctant	不情願的
dark	陰鬱的

★公正無私，正派

I am a brave and unselfish man.
我是一個勇敢且無私的人。

I am a calm, impartial and detached person.
我是一個行事沉穩，公正，超然的人。

I always give disinterested advice.
我總是給人公正超然的建議。

I am a decent person.
我是一個正直的人。
我很正派。

記憶關鍵：

decent 在一般口語中常用來作為「像樣的」意思。
比如說：The boy deserves a pair of decent sneakers.
（那個男孩應該要擁有一雙像樣的運動鞋。）

★有能力，有效率

I am very organized.
我組織性很強。

I have very competent knowledge in this business.
我在這個產業裡有非常具競爭力的知識。

I am capable of hard works.
我可以勝任辛苦的工作。

I am a very capable product manager.
我是一個很能幹的產品經理。

I am a fully capable piano tutor.
我是一個很有能力的鋼琴輔導老師。

I am always productive at work.
我工作總是很有成效。
我工作很有生產力。

I am a very effective and efficient learner.
我學東西很有效率。

I always work effectively.
我總是很有工作效率。

I always work efficiently.
我工作效率很高。

最簡單的英文自我介紹

記憶關鍵：

使用 effective 和 efficient 時，請特別注意到這兩個字意義上的差別。英文要說得道地，這一點點就是關鍵喔！

effective 有效的；所有的事情都完成了，就是「做對的事情」，to do right things。

efficient 效率高的；花 20%的時間先處理重要性高的工作，就是「用對的方法做事情」，to do things right。

相反性格的形容詞

incapable	無能的
incompetent	不勝任的
irresponsible	不負責任的

★節儉，勤奮，認真

I live in a frugal life.
我過著勤儉節約的生活。

I am diligent in my work.
我很勤奮工作。

I am a frugal, plain, and practical person.
我是一個勤儉，樸素，務實的人。

I advocate the virtue of hard-work and thrift.
我提倡認真工作和節儉的美德。

I spent many laborious hours on this job.
我在這個工作上花很多精力。

I am a responsible person.
I am pretty responsible
我是一個認真負責的人。

Working hard is one of my good points.
工作認真是我的優點之一。

相反性格的形容詞

uninformed	無知的，不學無術的
impatient	不耐煩的
merciless	冷酷無情的
indifferent	漠不關心的
unconcerned	不關心的
reluctant	不願意的

★積極，強勢

I love to take risks.
我喜歡冒險。

I used to be the decision maker.
我總是當決策者。

I am ambitious.
我是一個有野心的人。
我是一個企圖心很強的人。
我很有雄心。

I am an aggressive person.
I am aggressive.
我是一個積極的人。

I am pretty tough.
I am pretty strong.
我還滿強勢的。
我還滿嚴格的。
我還滿堅韌的。

I have strong ego.
我主觀意識很強烈。

I am a positive person.
我是一個積極正面的人。

I enjoy challenge.
我喜歡挑戰。

I have a dominant personality.

我的性格比較強勢。

I am a dominant person, but I am also loving, caring, and respectful.

我是一個支配慾很強的人，但同時我也有愛心，關心人，同時受人尊重。

· Chapter 4 ·

談個人基本資料
Personal Information

★個人資料

My name is Jenny Chen.
我的名字叫 Jenny Chen.

My friends call me J.
我朋友都叫我 J.

Just call me J.
叫我 J 就好了。

J is my nickname.
J 是我的暱稱。

I am 23 years old.
我今年23歲。

I was born on nineteen eighty-four（1984）, July forth.
我是1984年7月4日生。

I am a woman.
I am a female
我是個女人。

I am a man.
I am a male
我是個男人。

I am a 24-year-old woman.
I am a 24-year-old female.
我是一個24歲的女性。

最簡單的英文自我介紹

I am a 24-year-old man.
I am a 24-year-old male.
我是一個24歲的男性。

I am a female, 5'3", 100 lbs.
我是一位女性，五呎三吋高，100磅重。

I am only 5 feet tall.
我只有5呎高。

I am almost 180 centimeter.
我幾乎快180公分高。

I am 53 kilograms.
我體重53公斤。

記憶關鍵：

women   woman 的複數。

men   man 的複數。

female 及 male 複數在字尾加上 s 成為 females 及 males 即可。

★星座

What's your sign?
你的星座是什麼？

I am a Sagittarian.
I belong to Sagittarius.
我是射手座的人。

星座單字

Arise	白羊座，白羊座的人
Taurus	金牛座，金牛座的人
Gemini	雙子座，雙子座的人
Cancer	巨蟹座，巨蟹座的人
Leo	獅子座，獅子座的人
Virgo	處女座，處女座的人
Libra	天秤座
Libran	出身天秤座的人
Scorpio	天蠍座
Scorpion	出身天蠍座的人
Sagittarius	人馬座，射手座
Sagittarian	出身射手座的人
Capricorn	山羊座，魔羯座，魔羯座的人
Aquarius	水瓶座，水瓶座的人
Pieces	雙魚座
Piscean	出身雙魚座的人

★生肖

What animal sign were you born under?
你屬什麼？

I was born under the year of monkey.
我是猴年出生的。

生肖單字

rat	鼠
ox	牛
tiger	虎
rabbit	兔
dragon	龍
snake	蛇
horse	馬
sheep	羊
lamb	羊
monkey	猴
rooster	雞
chicken	雞
dog	狗
pig	豬
boar	豬

★ 血型

What's your blood type?
你是什麼血型？
你的血型是那一型？

I am type O.
我血型 O 型。

O positive.
O 型陽性。

O negative.
O 型陰性。

I am an A.
我是 A 型。

I am an AB.
我是 AB 型。

I am type B.
我是 B 型。

★生長背景，居住環境

I am from a small town.
我來自一個小鎮。

I am from a big city.
我來自一個大城市。

I was brought up in a farm.
我在一個農場長大。

I am an aboriginal.
我是一個原住民。

I live in the mountain.
我住在山裡面。

I came to the city when I was eight.
我八歲時來到城市生活。

I come from Taipei.
我來自台北。

I was born in Tainan.
我在台南出生。

I was born and raised in Taipei.
我在台北出生長大。

I was born in Taipei and raised in US.
我在台灣出生，在美國長大。

I'm a Chinese lady. I was raised in HK and went to university overseas.
我是一個中國女孩，在香港長大，後來到國外讀大學。

We have great foods, hospitable people and warm climate.
我們這裡有很棒的食物，好客的人們和宜人的天氣。
（用於介紹地方，譬如自己的家鄉…等）

People always give hearty welcome to visitors.
人們總是給觀光客最熱誠的歡迎。
（用於介紹地方，譬如自己的家鄉…等）

We will offer you a cordial reception.
我們會致上我們最熱誠的接待。
（用於介紹當地民情）

★婚姻狀況

What's your marital status?
你的婚姻狀況是什麼？

How many times have you been married?
你結過幾次婚？

I am married.
我已婚.

I am married to a foreigner.
我嫁給了外國人。
我娶了外國人。

I have a Japanese wife.
我有一個日本籍的妻子。

I am single.
我單身。

I am not married.
我還沒結婚。

My wife (or husband) and I are separated.
我跟我的妻子（或丈夫）分居了。

I am divorced.
我離婚了。

I remarried two years ago.
I married again two years ago.
我兩年前再婚。

I am widowed for two years.
I lost my wife (or husband) two years ago.
My wife (or husband) passed away two years ago.
I became a widower (or window) two years ago.
我兩年前喪偶。

I am widowed.
我配偶過世了。

I am a widower with two children.
我是一個鰥夫，帶著兩個小孩。（妻子過世）

I am a widow.
我是一個寡婦。（丈夫過世）

記憶關鍵：

marital status	婚姻狀況
spouse	配偶

★ 家庭狀況

How many children do you have?
How many kids do you have?
你有幾個小孩？

How many people are there in your family?
How many members are there in your family?
你家裡有多少成員？

I have a 7-year-old boy (or girl).
我有個七歲的兒子/女兒。

I have two kids.
我有兩個小孩。

I have two brothers and a sister.
我有兩個哥哥（或弟弟）和一個姐姐（或妹妹）。

I have a half brother.
我有一個同父異母（或是同母異父）的哥哥。

記憶關鍵：

half brother 或是 half sister 直接翻譯，就是「半個兄弟」，或「半個姐妹」，也就是同父異母（或是同母異父）的關係。同樣的方式也可以應用在父母親來自不同種族或國籍時，比如說：half-Chinese，就是指有中國血統的混血兒。

I'm half American and half Italian.
我是美國及義大利混血兒。

My parents are very religious.
我的父母篤信宗教。

I grow up in a patriotic family.
我在一個愛國意識強烈的家庭長大。

I come from a political family.
我來自一個政治世家。

My parents are both teachers.
我父母都是老師。

My parents and I live together.
我和父母同住。

My parents and I live next to each other.
我父母親和我住在隔壁。

My family lives in the same building.
我和家人住在同一棟房子裡。

I live along.
我自己一個人住。
我獨居。

I share a house with my friends.
我跟朋友合住一間屋子。

My father has retired.

我父親退休了。

My mother is a successful business woman.
我母親是一位成功的商場女強人。

I come from an ordinary family.
我來自一個平凡的家庭。

My families are very close.
我的家人感情很親密。

I come from a big family.
我來自一個大家庭。

I come from a warm family of 4 members.
我來自一個四人的溫暖家庭。

There are 4 members in my family.
我家有四個人。

My family is composed of 4 people.
我的家庭由四個人組成

We are a core family.
我來自一個核心家庭。
（及家庭成員僅有父母及小孩）

I come from a single parent family.
我來自一個單親家庭。

記憶關鍵：

family 接單數動詞時指「家庭」，接複數動詞時則指「家庭成員」。

描述父母的職業

housewife	家庭主婦
businessman	生意人
businesswoman	女性商業家，女強人
CPA; certified public accountant	會計師
accountant	會計
engineer	工程師
architect	建築師
politician	政治人物
doctor	醫生
nurse	護士
lawyer	律師
teacher	老師
farmer	農夫
volunteer	志工
postman	郵差
mechanist	機械技師
journalist	記者
actor	演員
actress	女演員
singer	歌手
work in show biz	在娛樂圈工作
work at home	在家工作
open his/her own shop	自己開店
own a shop	自己有一家店
run his/her own business	自己作生意
just an ordinary employer	只是一個普通的僱員

親屬稱謂

father	父親
mother	母親
husband	丈夫
wife	妻子
child / children	小孩子 / 小孩子（複數）
daughter	女兒
son	兒子
brother	兄弟
sister	姊妹
elder / younger brother	哥哥 / 弟弟
younger / elder sister	妹妹 / 姊姊
uncle	伯/叔/舅/姑/姨父
aunt	伯/叔/舅/姑/姨母
cousin	堂表兄弟姊妹
nephew	侄子
niece	侄女
father-in-law	公公
mother-in-law	婆婆
sister-in-law	嫂子/弟妹
brother-in-law	姊夫/妹夫
daughter-in-law	兒媳婦
son-in-law	女婿
great-grandparents	曾祖父母
grandparents	祖父母
grandfather	祖父
grandmother	祖母
granddaughter	孫女
grandson	外孫子

★基本健康狀況

I am under weight.
我體重過輕。

I am over weight.
我體重過重。

What's your vision?
你的視力狀況如何？

My vision is twenty-twenty （20/20）.
我的視力1.0。

I have very little vision.
我的視力很差。

I have little vision in my right eye.
我的右眼視力不好。

How strong are your glasses?
你近視多少度？

Minus 3 diopters.
-3D.
近視三百度。

Plus 3 diopters.
+3D.
遠視300度。

I have minus five diopters in myopia and additional minus 0.5 diopter of astigmatism.
我有500度近視和50度的散光。

I wear contact lenses.
I wear contacts.
我戴隱形眼鏡。

I've got myopia and astigmatism.
我是近視加散光。

I have near-sightedness.
I am a myopia.
我是個近視眼。
我有近視。

I am far-sighted.
I am a hyperopia.
我是個遠視眼。
我有遠視。

I am color-blind.
我有色盲。

I have heart disease, it's genetic.
I have inherited cardiac problem.
My family has heart problems, it's genetic.
我有心臟病，遺傳的。

I have hereditary disease.
I have genetic disease.
我有遺傳性疾病。

★外表及文化背景

I am an Asian woman.
我是一個亞洲女子。

I am an attractive girl with long straight hair and beautiful appearance.
我是一個迷人的女孩，長髮，五官漂亮。

I have good smile.
我的笑容不錯。

I am feminine.
我很女性化。

I have the feminine elegance of an Asian woman.
我有亞洲女性特有的嬌柔優雅氣質。

I am beautiful.
I am pretty.
我長的漂亮。

I am a cute girl.
我是一個可愛的女孩。

I am attractive.
我很有吸引力。

I am good looking.
我長的很好看。（形容男女性皆可）

I am very handsome.
我長很英俊。（形容男性）

I am charming.
我很迷人。

記憶關鍵：

charming 也可以用來形容個性。

I have brown eyes.
我有一雙深咖啡色的眼睛。

I am a brunet.
我是一個褐髮女子。

I am a blondie.
我是金髮碧眼的女人。

記憶關鍵：

brunet 及 blondie 是形容女子專用。形容男性時，單純使用 brown hair 及 blond hair 即可。

I have brown hair.
I have dark hair.
我頭髮是深（褐）色的。

I am a Caucasian.
我是白種人。

I am an African.
I am a black.
我是非裔黑人。（黑人）

Chapter

I am an Afro-American.
I am a black.
我是美籍非裔人士。（美國黑人）

I am a Latino.
我是拉丁裔人士。

I am an Asian.
我是亞裔人士。（黃種人）

各種體型

big	個頭很大
small	個頭小
beer belly	啤酒肚
overweight	超重的
fat	肥胖的
baby fat	嬰兒肥
chubby	豐滿，胖嘟嘟
thin	瘦瘦的
skinny	瘦的
slim	苗條
slender	修長苗條的
fit	體型剛好
tall	高的
short	矮的
ugly	醜的

heavy	重的
physique	體格，體型，多談男人的身材
figure	身材，多談女人的身材
macho	肌肉發達
muscular	肌肉發達
curvy figure	曲線玲瓏
stacked	曲線玲瓏

國籍和人種

race or ethnicity	種族
White, non-Hispanic	白人，非西班牙人
Black, non-Hispanic	黑人，非西班牙人
Caucasian	白種人
Hispanic	西班牙人
Latino	拉美洲人
Asian	亞洲人
Pacific Islander	太平洋群島人士
American Indian	印第安人
Native Alaskan	阿拉斯加原住民
African	非洲人，非洲的
American	美國人，美洲人，美國的，美洲的
Antarctic	南極的，南極地帶的
Australian	澳洲的，澳大利亞的，澳大利亞人
European	歐洲的，歐洲人的，歐洲人
North American	北美洲的
South American	南美洲的

國籍

America（美國）　　　　American（美國人）
Australia（澳大利亞）　　Australian（澳大利亞人）
Brazil（巴西）　　　　　Brazilian（巴西人）
Britain（英國）　　　　　British（英國人）
England（英國，英格蘭）　English（英國人）
Ireland（愛爾蘭）　　　　Irish（愛爾蘭人）
Canada（加拿大）　　　　Canadian（加拿大人）
China（中國）　　　　　　Chinese（中國人）
Taiwan（台灣）　　　　　Taiwanese（台灣人）
Egypt（埃及）　　　　　　Egyptian（埃及人）
France（法國）　　　　　French（法國人）
Germany（德國）　　　　　German（德國人）
Greece（希臘）　　　　　Greek（希臘人）
India（印度）　　　　　　Indian（印度人）
Israel（以色列）　　　　　Israeli（以色列人）
Italy（義大利）　　　　　Italian（義大利人）
Japan（日本）　　　　　　Japanese（日本人）
The Netherlands（荷蘭）　Dutch（荷蘭人）
New Zealand（紐西蘭）　　New Zealander（紐西蘭人）
Portugal（葡萄牙）　　　　Portuguese（葡萄牙人）
Russia（俄國）　　　　　Russian（俄國人）
Scotland（蘇格蘭）　　　Scots, Scottish（蘇格蘭人）
Spain（西班牙）　　　　　Spanish（西班牙人）
Sweden（瑞典）　　　　　Swedish（瑞典人）
Switzerland（瑞士）　　　Swiss（瑞士人）
Thailand（泰國）　　　　Thai（泰國人）
Philippines（菲律賓）　　Philippine（菲律賓人）
Vietnam（越南）　　　　　Vietnamese（越南人）

·Chapter 5·

談學習經歷
Education

★修習課程

My major is Business Administration.
Business Administration is my major.
我主修企管。

I major in Chinese literature and French.
我主修中國文學及法語。

I minor in Biology.
Biology is my minor.
我副修生物。

I major in French and minor in education.
我主修法文副修教育。

I am a dual major in marketing and journalism.
我雙主修行銷和新聞。

I am a dual major in Biology and Chemistry.
我雙主修生物及化學。

I graduated with a dual major in Mass-Communication and Sociology
我畢業於大眾傳播及社會學的雙主修學位。

I have completed my diploma in computer engineering.
我已經完成了電腦工程課程。
我以經從電腦工程科系畢業。

I completed my undergraduate studies with a dual major in Physics and Mathematics.
我完成了我的物理和數學雙主修學士學位。

I took a double major in Journalism and History.
我在學時是新聞及歷史雙主修。

I took a dual major in international relations and French language.
我在學時是國際關係和法文雙主修。

I plan to do dual major in Biology and Medicine.
我計畫雙主修生物及醫學。

I plan to pursue a dual field of concentration.
我計劃攻讀兩個領域。

I decide to dual major in a foreign language and diplomacy.
我決定雙主修外文和外交。

I was a history and biology dual major in college.
我唸書時雙主修歷史及生物。

I am an MBA student, concentrate in financial management.
我是一個企管碩士班的學生，專攻財務管理。

I plan to apply for a MBA, concentrate in Marketing.
我計劃申請就讀MBA，專攻行銷。

記憶關鍵：

dual major = double major	雙主修
major	主修
minor	副修
concentrate	專攻（某一學科）
field of concentration	攻讀學科

English is mandatory.
English is a mandatory course.
英文是必修課。

English is required.
English is a required course.
英文是必修課。

English is an obligatory course.
English is obligatory.
英文是必修課。

History is an elective.
History is optional.
History is an elective course.
歷史是一門選修課程。

I decide to take the elective.
我決定要選修這門課。

Although this is an optional course, I still decide to take it.
雖然這是一門選修課，我仍然決定要修它。

I took a course in Social Science Study.
我在學時選修了一門社會科學研究的課程。

I enrolled History.
我已選修了歷史。
我已註冊了歷史課

I took Japanese.
我選修過日文。

I went to the University of Birmingham for 3 month language course.
我曾去伯明罕大學上過三個月的語言課程。

I went to US for a summer to study English.
我去過美國一個暑假學習英文。

記憶關鍵：

optional = elective	選修科目，選修
mandatory = required	必修科目，必修
obligatory	必修的
take	選（某一課程）
enroll	註冊

數理科系名稱

Math, Mathematics	數學
Algebra	代數
Geometry	幾何
Science	科學，理科
Biology	生物
Chemistry	化學
Biochemistry	生物化學
Physics	物理
Medicine	醫學
Physical Geography	地球科學
Astronomy	天文學
Metallurgy	冶金學
Atomic Energy	原子能學
Chemical Engineering	化學工程
Engineering	工程學
Mechanical Engineering	機械工程學
Electronic Engineering	電子工程學

商學科系名稱

Commercial Science	商學
Economics	經濟學
Politics	政治學
Banking	銀行學
Accounting	會計學
Finance	財政學
Accounting and Statistics	會計統計
Business Administration	工商管理
Marketing	行銷學

文學科系名稱

Chinese	中文
English	英語
Japanese	日語
History	歷史
Geography	地理
Literature	文學
Linguistics	語言學
Library	圖書館學
Diplomacy	外交
Foreign Language	外文
Mass-Communication	大眾傳播學
Journalism	新聞學

其他科系名稱

Anthropology	人類學
Human Resource	人力資源
Sociology	社會學
Social science	社會科學
Psychology	心理學
Philosophy	哲學
Civil Engineering	土木工程
Architecture	建築學
Law, Jurisprudence	法學
Botany	植物
Agriculture	農學
Gymnastics	體育
Zoology	動物學
International Study	國際情勢
Culture Study	文化研究

★修習學位

I have a bachelor degree in Information Technology.
I have a BSc in Information Technology.
我有一個資訊學士學位。

I have a bachelor degree in Art.
I have a BA degree
我有一個文科學士學位。

I have a master degree in computer science.
I have a MSc. in Computer Science.
我有一個電腦科學碩士學位。

I have a PhD. degree in Biomedical Engineering.
我有一個生物醫學工程的博士學位。

I have a BA degree in Linguistics from the University of Victoria.
我有 Victoria 大學語言學系的文科學士學位。

I earned a BA degree in Art.
我擁有一個藝術學士學位。

I hold a Bachelor degree in Math.
我擁有一個數學學士學位。

I hold a joint degree in financial and Statistics.
我擁有金融及統計雙修學位。

I hold two BA degrees in Education and Psychology and an MSc degree. in Computer Science from the University of Waterloo.
我在 Waterloo 大學完成教育及心理學學位，還完成了一個電腦科學碩士學位。

During my MSc. in Information Technology, I also did Software Engineering.
在我讀資訊科技碩士期間，我也修了軟體工程。

I obtained an equivalent educational level.
我持有同等學力（歷）。

I am preparing to enter a master's program after completing my bachelor's degree.
在完成了學士課程後我準備讀碩士。

I am doing my Master's degree.
我正在攻讀碩士學位。

I am studying my Master's degree.
我正在攻讀碩士學位。

I have applied a degree program next semester.
我已經提出了下學期學位課程的入學申請。

記憶關鍵：

have = hold	擁有（某一學位）
obtain	獲得（某一學位）
complete	完成（某一學位）

學歷名稱

degree	學位
Bachelor	學士
Master	碩士
Doctor of Philosophy	博士
Associate Degree	副學士學位
A.A. Associate of Arts	文副學士
A.S. Associate of Science	理副學士
Bachelor Degree	學士學位
BA; Bachelor of Arts	文學士
BSc; Bachelor of Science	理學士
First Professional Degree	初級專業學位
MD; Doctor of Medicine	醫學士
JD; Juries Doctor	法學士
Master Degree	碩士學位
MA; Master of Arts	文學碩士
MSc.; Master of Science	科學碩士
MBA; Master of Business Administration	企管碩士
M.F.A.; Master of Fine Arts	藝術碩士
LL.M.; Master of Law	法學碩士
MED; Master of Education	教育碩士
Doctoral Degree	博士學位
Ph.D.; Doctor of Philosophy	哲學博士
J.S.D.; Doctor of Judicial Science	法學博士
D.Ed./Ed.D.; Doctor of Education	教育博士
D.Sc./Sc.D.; Doctor of Science	科學博士

★ 求學過程

I went to university overseas.
我在國外唸大學。

I completed my high school degree abroad.
I did my high school degree abroad.
我在國外完成我的高中學歷。

I've never studied abroad.
我從沒出國唸過書。

When I was 10, I was transferred to another school.
我十歲時被轉到另一家學校。

Because of my parent's job, I was transferring from school to school.
因為我父母工作的關係，我經常轉學。

I am home schooled.
我在家自學。

I plan to apply for a PhD program in two years.
我計畫兩年後申請博士課程。

My academic career at New York University was enriching.
我在紐約大學的求學生涯使我的人生更加豐富。

Throughout my academic career, I was very active.
在學習生涯中，我非常活躍。

I worked hard with my schoolwork and actively participated in extracurricular activities.
我對於課業非常認真，同時踴躍參與課外活動。

My academic career was a little bit special.
我的求學生涯有一點特殊。

After I graduated from high school, I chose a military career.
我高中畢業後選擇了軍旅生涯。

After I finished my military service, I decided to go back to school again.
我服完兵役後，決定再度回到學校唸書。

After graduated from college, I worked for 2 years.
大學畢業後，我工作了兩年。

Then I decided to pursue a master degree.
後來我決定攻讀碩士學位。

I was expelled from school.
I was dismissed from school.
我被學校退學。

I passed the university admission via screening and recommendation.
我通過大學入學推薦甄試。

I am a screen test candidate.
我被推薦參加甄試。

After my first year in business school, I did an internship in a financial department.
完成第一年商學系課程之後，我進入一家公司的財會部門

I was an intern of an international company.
我曾進入一家國際企業實習。

The company gave me a chance to visit Korea for an on job training.
這家公司給了我一個機會到韓國接受在職進修。

I was offered a chance to US for advance studies.
我有機會外派到美國去進修。

I passed the examination of government sponsorship for overseas study.
我通過了公費留學考試。

I was awarded scholarships sponsored by the government.
我獲得公費留學獎學金。

My undergraduate degree was completed through correspondence education.
我的大學教育是經由函授的方式完成的。

I studied at my own expense.
我自費唸書。

I was in the work-study program.
我是半工半讀的學生。

I was a part-time student.
我是兼職學生。

I was a full-time student.
我是全職學生。

記憶關鍵：

screen test	甄試
oral test	口試
advance study	進修
additional training	進修
further study	進修
further training	進修
further education	進修
public expense	公費
government scholarship	公費
government sponsorship	政府贊助，公費
at one's own expense	自費
support oneself	自己負擔費用
free education	免費義務教育
compulsory education	義務教育
mandatory education	義務教育
education of adolescence	青春期教育
adolescent education	青少年教育
teenager education	青少年教育
general education	中學教育
secondary education	中學教育
advanced education	高等教育
adult education	成人教育
equal education	同等學力
correspondence education	函授教育
full-time education	全日制教育
part-time education	非全日制教育
regular education	正規教育

For personal reasons, I dropped out of school when I was 20.
因為某些個人因素，我20歲時不得不放下學業。

I left school when I was 20, for personal reasons.
我20歲時因為個人因素離開學校。

I quit high school because I had to take care of my mother, who was really sick.
為了照顧我病重的母親，我不得不放下高中學業。

For economic reason, I was not allowed to continue my academic career.
因為經濟上的因素，我無法繼續學業。

記憶關鍵：

cut school	翹課，曠課
drop school, drop out	輟學
quit school	輟學
expel from school	開除，退學
dismiss from school	退學
leave school	休學，或因任何理由離開學校

★學業成績

My hard work landed me at the top of my class.
我努力讀書的成果使我的成績在班上名列前茅。

I was awarded a science scholarship.
我得到了科學獎獎學金。

I was one of the outstanding students.
我是成績頂尖的學生之一。

I had good grades at school.
我在學校得到很好的成績。

I have to admit that I am not a good student.
我必須承認我不是一個好學生。
我必須承認我書讀的不是很好。

I wasn't a smart student, but I worked really hard.
我不是一個聰明的學生，但我很認真。

I had a poor grade at school.
我在校成績不好。

My school works were barely satisfied.
我的在校成績中下。

I was entitled to a first degree after two years as an under-graduate student.
我大學第二年就得到學士學位。

記憶關鍵：

first degree = bachelor's degree	大學學位
second degree = master's degree	碩士學位
outstanding	傑出
good	優良
pass	及格
just satisfied	中等
barely satisfied	中下
fail	不及格，可補考
incomplete	不完整的，重修
make-up test	補考

★專業考試

I attended Civil Service Exam two years ago.
我兩年前參加過公職考試。

I've passed CPA exam.
我通過了會計師考試。

I attended public exam.
我參加國家考試。

I signed up various exams.
我報名了各式各樣的考試。

記憶關鍵：

Senior Civil Service Exam	高考
Junior Civil Service Exam	普考
Special Civil Service Exam	特考
Civil Service	文官，文職
Qualified Exam	資格考試
Preliminary Exam	檢定考試
CIA Exam	稽核師考試
CFA Exam	財務分析師考試
Grade C test	丙級考試
Grade B test	乙級考試
Grade A test	甲級考試

I attended GEPT test.
我參加過全民英檢。

I passed High Intermediate GEPT test.
我通過了中高級英檢。

記憶關鍵：

GEPT; General English Proficiency Test	全民英檢
Elementary Certificate	初級證照
Intermediate Certificate	中級證照
High-Intermediate Certificate	中高級證照
Advanced Certificate	高級證照

★ 學歷

I am a collage student.
我現在是大學生。

I am a high school student.
我是個高中生。

I am a graduate student.
我是個研究生。

I just graduated from Taiwan University this June.
我今年六月剛從台灣大學畢業。

I am about to graduate from collage.
我即將大學畢業。

I am going to graduate from collage in two month.
我再兩個月就大學畢業了。

I am about to leave school.
我即將離開學校（畢業）。

I am going to graduate from New York University, School of Business.
我即將從紐約大學商學院畢業。

I will receive a graduation certificate with doctoral degree in 2 months.
我即將在兩個月內得到博士學位的畢業證書。

I graduated from Taiwan University two years ago.
我兩年前從台灣大學畢業。

記憶關鍵：

Doctoral Candidate	博士候選人
PhD Candidate	博士候選人
Viva-voce	呈交論文時必需通過的論文答辯，論文口試
oral test	口試
graduate	研究生
postgraduate	研究生
undergraduate	大學生
college student	大學生

★概談曾受過的教育

I am well educated.
我很有教養的。
（我受過不錯的教育。）

I've never received advance education, but I have worthy experience.
我雖沒有接受過高等教育，但我有很多珍貴的經驗。

I went to nice schools.
我從很好的學校畢業。

I attended many seminars.
我參加過許多研討會。

I was home schooled.
我在家自學。

·Chapter 6·

談工作經歷
Work Experience

★最簡單的職業類別自我介紹

What is your occupation?
你的職業是什麼？

I am a _____ .
我是一個_____。
以上空格部份，可置入以下職業類別。
若第一個字母為母音，則冠詞「a」改為 an。

娛樂及傳播事業

actor	男演員
actress	女演員
anchor	新聞主播
announcer	廣播員
clown	小丑
TV producer	電視製作人
singer	歌手
movie director	導演
movie star	電影明星
model	模特兒
magician	魔術師

旅遊餐廳休閒百貨業

bell boy	門童
bellhop	旅館的行李員
bin man	清潔工，垃圾工
desk clerk	接待人員
baker	烘培師
cook	廚師
chef	廚師
waiter	侍者（服務生）
waitress	女侍者（服務生）
baseball player	棒球選手
boxer	拳擊手
athletic	運動員
masseur	男按摩師
masseuse	女按摩師
guide	導遊
tour guide	導遊
cashier	出納
clerk	店員
receptionist	櫃台接待人員

需特殊技術的職業

photographer	攝影師
seamstress	女裝裁縫師
tailor	裁縫師
barber	理髮師（男）
hairdresser	理髮師，美容師（女）
driver	司機
cobbler	鞋匠
carpenter	木匠
farmer	農夫
fisherman	漁夫
florist	花商
gardener	花匠，園丁
blacksmith	鐵匠
miner	礦工
dustman, janitor	清潔工
butcher	屠夫，肉商
construction worker	建築工人
electrician	電工
mechanic	機械師，機修工
technician	技術人員
welder	焊接工
auto mechanic	汽車技工
repairman	修理工人

較具專業性質的工作類別

CPA	會計師
auditor	審計員
architect	建築師
judge	法官
lawyer	律師
associate professor	副教授
professor	教授
scientist	科學家
musician	音樂家
mathematician	數學家
geologist	地質學家
statistician	統計學家
artist	藝術家
dancer	舞者
cartoonist	漫畫家
astronaut	太空人
teacher	教師
priest	牧師
flight attendant	空服員
airline representative	地勤人員
pilot	飛行員，飛機駕駛員
computer programmer	程式師

detective	偵探
engineer	工程師
designer	設計師
dentist	牙科醫生
doctor	醫生
vet	獸醫
veterinarian	獸醫
nurse	護士
pharmacist	藥劑師

其他事業

guard	警衛
life guard	救生員
housekeeper	管家
housewife	家庭主婦
operator	接線生
nun	尼姑
monk	和尚，教士
real estate agent	房地產經紀人
broker / agent	經紀人
librarian	圖書管理員
volunteer	志工
social worker	社會福利工作者

★ 工作經歷

I have been in the employ of an exporting company for over two years.
我曾經受雇於出口貿易公司超過兩年。
我曾在出口貿易公司工作超過兩年。

For the past four years, I have been working for S&E Co.
過去四年我受雇於 S&E 公司。

I have been employed by S&E Co. for almost 5 years.
I have been employed for almost 5 years by S&E Co.
I worked with S&E for almost 5 years.
我在 S&E 公司工作超過五年。

I have had one year experience with S&E Co as an intern.
I worked at S&E Co. as an Intern for one year.
I was an intern at S&E Co. for one year.
我在 S&E 公司有過一年實習的經驗。

I have three years experience in sales and marketing in manufacturing environment.
我有三年以上製造業市場及銷售經驗。

I was just a messenger when I started working in S&E Co.
我剛進 S&E 公司時，只負責文件遞送的工作。

I also have 2 years experience in manufactory industry with similar customers.
我也有兩年製造業相關經驗。

I was promoted to a senior financial analyst in two years.
我在兩年內就被升職為資深財務分析師。

I worked in a restaurant for a summer.
我有一年暑假期間曾在餐廳打工。

I am a full-time student as well as a yoga teacher at night.
我白天是一個全職學生，晚上是瑜珈老師。

I am very experienced with the principles of design.
我對於設計的準則很有實戰經驗。

I have very specific experiences in this field.
我在這個領域有具體的經驗。

I was the chairman (or a member) of student committee.
我曾擔任學生會的主席（成員）之一。

I was the president (or a member) of Science society.
我曾擔任科學研究社的社長（社員）。

I wrote a story about this field.
我寫過關於這個領域的文章。

I did a lot research on this area.
我在這個部份做了很多研究。

記憶關鍵：

experience	經歷，經驗
work experience	工作經歷
work history	工作經歷
previous employment	工作經歷
employment history	工作經歷
employment record	工作經歷，受雇紀錄
business experience	工作經歷
business background	工作經歷
professional	職業經歷
business history	工作經歷
specific experience	具體經歷
professional experience	工作經歷
employer	雇主
employee	雇員，受雇者
period	期間
period of employment	服務期間
promote	升職

★工作職掌

I am in charge of China market.
我負責中國大陸市場。

I help to prepare the sales annual budget.
我協助年度銷售計畫的建立。

I also handle the import & export affairs.
我也負責進出口事務。

I focus on the market research.
我專門負責市場研究。

I am responsible for the Public Relationship.
我負責公關工作。

I am responsible to the on-site or off-site training.
我負責現場或遠端的培訓活動。

I am responsible to replenish the stock.
我負責把倉庫補滿。

I make sure all shipments are delivered on time.
我負責讓所有貨物都能準時遞送。

I deal with all customer issues.
我處理所有客戶提出的需求。

Except finance, I basically cover everything.
除了財務之外，我幾乎囊括了所有工作。

It is my responsibility to dig out the real issue.
發掘出真正的問題點是我的責任。

I am in charge of buying and selling.
我負責買及賣。

I assist new customer development and marketing plan.
我協助新客戶及市場計畫的開發。

I make sure the quality remains perfect.
我負責使品質維持完美。

I assist to set up distribution channels.
我協助建立分銷管道。

I perform related duties as assigned.
我負責執行所有被指派的任務。

I have to maintain the existing accounts as well as new account development.
我必須負責處理現有客戶的需求同時開發新客戶。

記憶關鍵：

be responsible for/to	負責
handle	處理
deal with	處理
present employment	現職狀況
responsibility	工作職掌
type of work	工作性質
employment	工作
duty	職責
administer	管理
appointed	被任命
assist	輔助
export	出口
import	進口

★ 工作時間

I work full-time.
I work on a full-time job.
I have a full-time job.
我是正職員工。

I work from nine to six everyday.
我每天從九點工作到五點。

I have a part-time job.
我有一個兼職工作。

I work on a part-time job.
我是兼職員工。

I work on contract.
I work on contract basis.
我是派遣員工。
我依契約期間工作。

I am on duty.
I am working.
我在上班。
我在值班。

I am off duty.
I am off work.
我下班了。

I work in a hotel, the reception must be available around the clock.
我在旅館工作，櫃檯必須隨時有人。

I am required to be on call.
我被要求要能夠隨傳隨到。

記憶關鍵：

| around the clock | 日以繼夜的 |
| on call | 隨傳隨到 |

I can switch shift with you.
I can swap shift with you.
我可以跟你換班。

I work the night shift.
I take the night shift.
我上夜班。

I work in shift.
我的工作是輪班制。

I can take over her shift.
我可以為她代班。

I work two shifts.
我連上兩個班次。（為了多賺一點錢或是為人代班…等原因）

記憶關鍵：

day shift = first shift	早班，白天的時間上班。
swing shift = second shift	中班，下午到晚上的時間上班。
night shift = third shift	晚班，小夜班，晚上上班。
graveyard shift	大夜班，子夜至清晨上班。
time-shifted schedule	班表
employment schedule	班表
shift work	輪班制
shift system	輪班系統
clock off = clock out = punch out	打卡下班
clock on = clock in = punch in	打卡上班
on duty	值班中
off duty	下班

★ 工作地點

I worked in China.
我在中國大陸工作過。

I am willing to relocate to China.
我很樂意被派駐到中國大陸工作。

I am willing to travel to job-site.
我很樂意依工作需求出差。

I prefer to stay in Taipei, but I can work in China, too.
我比較喜歡留在臺北工作，但我也可以到中國大陸去。

I've been working in US for 2 years.
我曾在美工作兩年。

I worked in Singapore for almost 2 months.
我曾在新加坡工作過兩個月。

I worked for Taiwan office for two years, and then I was
sent to headquarter in US for a training.
我在台灣分公司待了兩年，然後被派到美國總公司去培訓。

I work at home.
我在家工作。

I work on the street.
我在外執行勤務。（工作性質為必須在街上值勤的工作）

I have a desk job.
我做的是辦公室內勤工作。

I work in the field.
我做的是外勤工作。

I travel around the world for business.
我為了工作必需行遍全世界。

I work off-site.
我到外部區域工作。
（因工作需要，到自家公司以外的地方提供服務）

I provide off-site service.
我提供外派服務。

I provide door-to-door service.
我提供到府服務。

★部門及職稱

I enlisted in the army.
我從軍。

I am a freelancer.
我不受雇於任何公司，是自由業者。
我是獨立工作者。

I am a freelance designer.
我是獨立工作的設計師

I am a nurse.
我是一個護士。

記憶關鍵：

這是說明自己目前工作最基本的句子。以上句中，護士
（nurse）可以置換為您目前所從事的任何工作。不管在或不
在職場上，都可以使用這個句型。
記得，在職稱前面務必加上冠詞 a 或 an。
比如說：
I am a teacher. 我是一個老師。
I am a house wife. 我是一個家庭主婦。
I am a student. 我是一個學生。
I am a business man. 我是個生意人。

I am an assistant engineer in S&E Co.
我在 S&E 公司擔任助理工程師。

I am the President & General Manager of S&E Co.
我是 S&E 公司的總裁兼總經理。

記憶關鍵：

到底什麼時候用冠詞 a/an 或是冠詞 the 呢？簡單説，a/an 用來説明「非特定的人或物」，相對的 the 就是用在説明「特定的人或物」時。以上句中，the 強調 S&E Co 公司中唯一的總裁兼總經理職位，故用 the President & General Manager。

I'm working as a nurse.
我的工作是一個護士。
我以護士為職。

I am working as a sales representative in S&E Co.
我在 S&E 公司擔任業務代表。

記憶關鍵：

work as 通常與職場上的職稱連用，當然也要記得加上冠詞 a 或 an。比如説：I work as an accountant 我以會計師為職。

常見部門稱謂：

Business Division	營業部，事業處
Business Unit	營業部，事業處
General Affairs Department	總務部
Financial Department	財務部
Human Resources Department（HR）	人力資源部
Personnel Department	人事部
Accounting Department	會計部
Sales Department	銷售部
Marketing Department	行銷部
Advertising Department	廣告部
Planning Department	企劃部
Public Relations Department（PR）	公共關係部門
Product Development Department	產品開發部
International Department	國際部，海外部門
Shipping Department	船務部門
Import Department	進口部門
Export Department	出口部門
Research and Development Department（R&D）	
	研發部
Branch Office	分公司
Head Office	總公司

常見辦公室職稱：

position	職位
job title	職位
Chairman	總裁
Vice Chairman	副總裁
President	董事長
Vice President	副董事長
General Manager（GM）	總經理
Vice President（VP）	副總經理
Chief Executive Officer（CEO）	執行長
Chief Financial Officer（CFO）	財務長
Chief Information Officer（CIO）	資訊長
Chief Knowledge Officer（CKO）	知識長
Chief Operating Officer（COO）	營運長
Chief Technology Officer（CTO）	技術長
Consultant	顧問
Adviser	顧問
Special Assistant	特別助理
Factory Chief	廠長
Factory Sub-Chief	副廠長
Director	協理
Assistant Vice President	協理
Director	處長

Vice Director	副處長
Manager	經理
Assistant Manager	副理
Junior Manager	襄理
Section Manager	課長
Deputy Section Manager	副課長
Supervisor	主任
Team Leader	組長
Administrator	管理師
Accountant	會計
Auditor	稽核
Engineer	工程師
Chief Engineer	首席工程師
Advisory Engineer	顧問工程師
Principle Engineer	策劃工程師
System Engineer	系統工程師
Project Leader Engineer	主任工程師
Account Engineer	專案工程師
Senior Engineer	高級工程師
Deputy Engineer	副工程師
Assistant Engineer	助理工程師
Assistant	助理
Clerk	事務員
Operator	作業員

Representative	代表
Secretary	秘書
Staff	職員
personnel	職員
Senior Specialist	高級專員，資深專員
Specialist	專員
Senior Technician	高級技術員，資深技術員
Technician	技術員
Assistant Technician	助理技術員
Team Leader	領班
Web Master	網站管理專員
Assistant	助理
maintenance worker, janitor	工友
contract employee	約聘人員
messenger	文件遞送員
temporary worker	臨時人員
substitute civilian serviceman	替代役男
contractor	承包商
PR, public relationship	公關（人員）
office staff	職員，上班族
buyer	採購
salesman, salesperson	業務
door-to-door salesman	推銷員

★ 曾參與的重要事務、工作成就或外派出差

I participated in the annual electronic equipment seminar.
我曾參加年度電子設備研討會。

During the past two years, I have made a 76% increase of revenue from \$10 million to \$18 million.
在過去兩年間，我使業績增加了75%，從一千萬到一千八百萬。

I got promoted in two years.
我在兩年內獲得升職。

I initiated the project and successfully win the case.
我提出了這項方案並成功贏得這個案子。

I created 70% profit.
我創造了70%的利潤。

I was assigned to handle this merge.
我被指定主持這次兩家公司的合併。

I was designated to lead the meeting.
我被選定主持這次的會議。

The project went perfectly on my watch.
在我的監督之下，該專案進行得非常完美。

I presented this joint venture policy to acquire the business interest.
我建議了該項合資方案使企業獲得應有的利潤。

I represented the S&E Co. to the US exhibition.
我代表 S&E 公司到美國參展。

I traveled to Iraq to gain more orders.
我出差到伊拉克以獲得更多的訂單。

I developed 30% new customers.
我開發了30%的新客戶。

I precisely controlled customer activities and competitor information.
我精準地掌控了客戶動態及競爭者訊息。

I built up standard work flow.
我制定了標準工作流程。

I reorganized the structure.
我把整個結構都重新整頓了一次。

★所從事的行業類別

I am engaged in retail trade.
我從事零售業。

I devote myself to the insurance business.
我從事保險業。

I am in the logistic business.
我在物流業。

I am an exporter/importer.
我是一個出口商/進口商。

I open my own shop.
我自己開店。

I own a restaurant.
我自己開餐廳。

I run my own business.
I have my own business.
我有自己的事業
我自己當老闆。

記憶關鍵：

不想詳細說明工作類別是哪一種時，以 run my own business
替代可以了。

I am self employed.
I am a freelancer.
我是自由業。

I work by case.
我自行接案工作。
我是自由業。

I work at home.
我在家工作。

I inherit a family business.
我繼承家業。

I work in family business.
我在自家開的公司裡工作。

I work for the government.
我在公家機關工作。

I work in a local company.
我在本地公司上班。

I work in a foreign company.
我在外商公司上班。

I work in a library.
我在圖書館工作。

記憶關鍵：

以上例句中，library 可置換成各種工作場所。比如說：

supermarket	超級市場
school	學校
restaurant	餐廳
locally-owned enterprise	私人企業
government-owned enterprise	公營企業
foreign-owned enterprise	外商公司
foreign company	外商公司
US-based company	美商公司
NGO; non government organization	非政府機構
charity institution	慈善團體
organization	公司團體
institution	公共團體，協會
Co. = company	公司，商號
enterprise	企業

行業類別單字：

dealer	經銷商
wholesale	批發
wholesaler	批發商
retailer	零售商
tradesman	零售商
middleman	中間商，經紀人
manufacturer	製造商，製造廠
local industry	地方工業
light industry	輕工業
power industry	電力工業
car industry	汽車工業
clothing industry	服裝業
building industry	建築工業
chemical industry	化學工業
food industry	食品工業
oil industry	石油工業
insurance business	保險業
insurance industry	保險業
communication industry	通訊業

★薪資及福利

I obtained shares of the company.
我獲得公司配股。

I was offered stock option.
我曾獲得認購股票的機會。

I got a nice bonus from the company.
公司給我不錯的紅利。

I also have a nice salary.
我也有不錯的薪水。

I think I deserve more salary.
我想我應該的到更多的薪水。

I am allowed 10 days off per year.
依規定我每年有10天假。

I get raises every year.
我年年都有加薪。

I work on contract, I do not qualify for any company benefits.
我依合約辦事，不適用於任何公司福利條款。

★職位上應具有的特點為何

I am able to work as a team.
我能夠與人團隊合作。

I have excellent communication skills.
我有優秀的溝通技巧。

I am an organized person.
我是一個很有組織性的人。

I am a logical person.
我很有邏輯性。

I can integrate multiple requirements swiftly.
我可以在很短的時間內整合許多需求。

I can work under stress.
我可以在壓力下工作。

I always accomplish my mission in limit time frame.
我總是在限定時間內完成所有的工作。

I always plan ahead.
我總是事先計畫好所有的事情。

I enjoy challenges.
我喜歡挑戰。

I can handle emergencies.
我能夠處理緊急事務。

I conclude issues quickly.
我可以很快的總結出問題重點。

I have a lot of connections.
我很有關係。

I am very diplomatic.
我很有交際手腕。

I can coordinate between departments.
我可以協調部門間的合作。

I am calm and sophisticated.
我冷靜且機靈。

★什麼經驗都沒有的話怎麼辦

I don't have any experience, but I am a fast learner.
我沒有什麼經驗，但我學得很快。

I don't have experiences in related field, but I work very hard.
我沒什麼相關經驗，但我工作非常認真。

I am finding a suitable company for an internship within the field of my study.
我在找一個合適的公司，可提供與我的研究範圍相關的實習機會。

· Chapter 7 ·

談人生經歷及生涯規畫
Career Plan

★人生的轉折點

I was not a top student until I met Mr. Lee.
在遇見李老師前，我並不是個好學生。

With Mr. Lee's encouragement, I started learning piano.
在李老師的鼓勵下，我開始學鋼琴。

It was a turning point of my life.
那是我人生的一個轉折點。

This setback bears a little impact on me.
這個挫折對我產生了一些衝擊。

I experienced a great change in my sophomore year.
我在大學二年級時經歷了一項轉變。

記憶關鍵：

freshman	大一新生
sophomore	指大二學生
junior	指大三學生
senior	指大四學生

★家庭經歷

My parents are my role model.
我的父母親是我的榜樣。

My beloved grandmother was our mentor.
我親愛的祖母是家裡的良師。

記憶關鍵：

以過去式呈現表示祖母已過世

I was born in an ordinary family.
我在一個平凡的家庭長大。

I live in a well-off family.
我生活在一個經濟狀況還不錯的家庭。

記憶關鍵：

well-off = well-to-do（經濟上）富裕的，寬裕的，也可以解釋為家中什麼都有，吃穿不用愁的「小康」家庭。

My parents were always not around.
我父母親經常不在身邊。

My sister passed away when I was 20.
我20歲時，我的妹妹過世了。

My childhood was spent with my grandparents.
我的童年是與我的祖父母一起度過的。

I don't have parents.
我沒有父母。
我是孤兒。

I was always on the move
我過去總是在搬家。

I wouldn't consider myself lucky .
我一向不認為自己幸運。

My parents have a great influence on me. With their guidance,
I am able to look at things in prospective.
我父母的言行對我影響重大，有了他們的導引，我能夠用正確
的眼光來看待所有事物。

Owing to my father's job, I was moving from school to school.
因為我父親工作的關係，我經常轉學。

My childhood hadn't been really happy.
我的童年過的並不快樂。

My family used to be very poor.
我的家過去非常窮。

We are a modest family.
我們家是一個小康家庭。

My grandmother is quite well-off.
我祖母非常富有。

My parents set a good example to us.
我的父母為我們樹立了很好的榜樣。

I have a correct attitude toward my life.
我對人生的態度很正面。

★出國經歷

I have been traveling all over the world.
我曾到過全世界許多國家。

I've seen a lot of poor people in Africa.
我在非洲見過很多窮苦人家。

I volunteered to work in France.
我自願到法國去工作。

When I was young, I used to join summer camps in Canada.
我小時候經常參加加拿大的夏令營。

I joined study tour every year.
我每年都出國遊學。

I've never left Taiwan.
我從沒出過國。
我從沒離開過台灣。

I was relocated to China.
我曾被派駐大陸。

★克服失敗獲得成功的經歷

I worried about a lot of things.
我總是感到擔憂。

I was always anxious about everything.
我總是不停的在憂慮著各種各樣的事情。

I was nervous to death and nearly gave in.
我緊張的要死，幾乎要讓步了。

I don't want to give up.
我不想放棄。

I overcame every difficulty and I did everything as best as I could to achieve the goal.
我克服了所有困難，並且盡全力達成目標。

After this tragedy, I became stronger.
這次的悲劇之後，我變得比較堅強。

I tried to pick up myself and deal with most of the problems in my daily life.
我試著振作自己，重新處理每天發生的問題。

I know how to pull myself together and try again.
我了解了應該怎麼找回自己並且再接再厲。

I decided to take the risk by starting my own business.
我決定要冒險創業。

I make sure I am well-informed.
我設法讓自己消息靈通。

最簡單的英文自我介紹

After my grandmother's death, I decided to contribute myself to the society.
在我祖母去世後，我決定將自己奉獻給社會。

After this failure, I stopped all experiments.
這次失敗後，我便停止了所有的實驗。

Nine months later, I started to employ another method.
九個月後，我開始嘗試另一種方法。

Chapter

★從參與的活動中啟發感想

This book made a great impact on me.
這本書對我造成了莫大的影響。

Through this seminar, I have learned how to work effectively with the team.
經過這次的研討會，我學會了一個團隊該如何有效的運作。

I learned critical techniques from this valuable experience.
經由此次寶貴的經驗，我學到了關鍵的技術。

The most valuable lesson I learn is "When you examine failure, you open the door to success."
我所學到最寶貴的一課是「當你開始反省失敗的同時，便幫自己開啟了通往成功之門。」

This failure made me even more interested in cancer research.
這項失敗使我對癌症研究更有興趣。

★未來發展方向及生涯規劃

I think it is a good choice for me to major in Science.
我想主修科學對我而言是一個不錯的選擇。.

I would like to go back to school for an EMBA degree.
我想要回到學校修習 EMBA 課程。

I think a sound system of internal control is essential to a company.
我認為完整的內控系統對於整個公司很重要。

I am interested in developing more about this task.
我對進一步發展這個主題很有興趣。

I am interested in developing ideas.
我對開發新概念很有興趣。

I have great interest in XX field.
我對 XX 領域有很強烈的興趣。

Hope this training will provide me with an insight into the future of web design.
希望這項訓練使我對未來網頁設計有更加深刻的理解。

I plan to work as a volunteer.
我計劃做一位志工。

I would like to become a real fashion designer in 3 years.
我想在三年內成為一位真正的時尚設計師。

My short term goal is to graduate from high school.
我的短期計畫是完成我的高中學業。

My mid-term goal is to become a certified public accountant.
我的中程計畫是成為一位有證照的公眾會計師。

My long-term goal is to become a top executive officer.
我的長期計畫是成為一位高階經理人。

After my graduation, I would like to apply for a job in design field.
畢業後我想找個與設計相關的工作。

I hope to become a professional in counseling education.
我希望變成一位從事輔導教育的專業人士。

I hope to become a professional baseball player.
我希望能成為一位職業棒球運動員。

I hope to become a student again.
我希望再度成為一個學生。

I would like to go back to school.
我希望再度回到學校。

I want to become a student of this Academy.
我想成為這個學院的一員。

I want to open a restaurant.
我希望可以開一家餐廳。

I want to have three kids.
我希望生三個小孩。

I would like to start my own family.
我想建立自己的家庭。

★表達信念及看法

I believe life is full of blessing.
我相信生命是上帝的恩賜。

I cherish the chance to establish a long term relationship with the right person.
我珍惜與適合的人一同建立長久關係的機會。

I hope we can share the happiness and sorrow together.
我希望我們可以一同分享所有的喜悅與憂傷。

It is my belief that the more efforts I make, the more progress I will achieve.
我深深相信努力得越多,進步得越多。

★常用的鼓勵式短語

Do your best.
Try your best.
盡力去做。

Keep going!
繼續努力。

Pluck up your sprit!
振作精神！

Never give up!
千萬別放棄！

Move on, you can make it!
繼續前進，你一定可以做到！

Work hard, play hard.
努力工作，用力的玩。

Truth fears no trial.
真金不怕火煉

Where there is a will, there is a way.
有志者，事竟成。

· Chapter 8 ·

專長及嗜好
Special Skills and Hobbies

★嗜好

What is your hobby?
你的嗜好是什麼？

Do you have any hobby?
你有沒有什麼嗜好？

What do you do in your spare time?
你空閒時都做什麼？

I have various pastimes.
我有很多不同的消遣。

I have various hobbies.
我有很多種嗜好。

I enjoy surfing.
我喜歡浮潛。

I play baseball.
我打棒球。

I am a skilled basketball player.
我對打籃球很在行。

I go shopping.
我逛街。

I am very interested in traveling and reading.
我十分喜愛旅行和閱讀。

I go mountain climbing every week.
我每週都去爬山。

I enjoy reading many kinds of books.
我喜歡閱讀各式各樣的書籍。

I like to watch TV.
我喜歡看電視。

I listen to music.
我聽音樂。

Beautiful melody comforts me..
美麗的旋律的撫慰我的心靈。

I go see movies.
I go to movies.
I go for movies.
I enjoy movies.
我去看電影。/ 我喜歡看電影。

I write sometimes.
我有時會寫作。

I play piano.
我彈鋼琴。

I have a fondness for painting.
我喜歡畫畫。

I go to karaoke.
我去唱卡啦 OK。

I practice boxing.
我練拳擊。

I practice karate.
我練空手道。

I go to the gym.
我去健身房。

I work out everyday.
I exercise everyday.
我每天運動。

I exercise regularly.
我有固定運動的習慣。

Exercise helps to maintain a strong body.
運動可以維持身體的強健。

Music helps to maintain a healthy mind.
音樂可以保持心理的健康。

I like chatting with friends over the internet.
我喜歡跟朋友在網路上聊天。

My favorite recreation activity is meeting friends for a pleasant dinner.
我最喜歡的休閒活動是和朋友相約去吃一頓愉快的晚餐。

最簡單的英文自我介紹

※「go」多半用在表示「做」戶外休閒嗜好或活動。代表休閒
活動的單字如果是動詞的話,記得加上 ing。

I go _____ ing.
我玩/做(某活動)。

I go jogging.
我去慢跑。

I go skating.
我去滑冰。

I go swimming.
我去游泳。

breaststroke	蛙式
backstroke	仰式
freestyle	自由式
butterfly	stroke 蝶式

※ 用「love 或 enjoy」表達自己嗜好時,後面的空格幾乎可以置
入以下任何詞語。另外,「fond of」也同樣是喜歡的意思。
代表活動的單字如果是動詞的話,記得加上 ing。

I enjoy _____ .
I love _____ .
I am fond of _____ .
(我喜歡_____。)

I enjoy jogging.
I love jogging.
我喜歡慢跑。

＊「彈奏」樂器
以下嗜好使用 play ＋ 樂器名稱。

I play _____.
（我玩某樂器。）

與 enjoy 連用時，改為 I enjoy playing _____。

violin	小提琴
viola	中提琴
cello	大提琴
keyboard	鍵盤
piano	鋼琴
organ	風琴
bass drum	大鼓
tambourine	鈴鼓，手鼓
drum machine	電子鼓
erhu	二胡
lute	琵琶
gu zheng	古箏

＊「做」運動
以下運動多用 do ＋ 運動名稱。
I do _____.
（我做___。）

push-up	伏地挺身
sit-up	仰臥起坐
weightlifting, weight training	舉重，重量訓練
aerobics	有氧舞蹈
step aerobics	階梯有氧

最簡單的英文自我介紹

※「從事」舞蹈活動
以下單字使用 go + Ving 或 enjoy + Ving 皆可。

I go ＿＿ing.
（我從事＿＿＿。）

I enjoy ＿＿＿ing.
（我喜歡＿＿＿。）

ballroom dancing	社交舞
American smooth	美國式的社交舞
Modern dance	摩登舞
Latin dance	拉丁舞
Rumba	倫巴
Cha-cha-cha	恰恰恰
Samba	森巴
Paso Double	鬥牛舞
Jive	捷舞，牛仔舞
Rock'n Roll dance	搖滾舞
folk dance	土風舞
belly dance	肚皮舞
flamingo	佛朗明哥
Mambo	曼波
Bolero	波麗露舞曲
Two Step	兩步舞
Hustle	哈斯爾
Salsa	騷莎
Argentine Tango	阿根廷探戈
belly dance	肚皮舞

＊「從事」球類運動
使用 play ＋ 運動名稱。表示從事某項運動的意思。

I play ＿＿＿＿。
（我從事＿＿＿＿。）

與 enjoy 連用時，改為
I enjoy playing ＿＿＿＿。
（我喜歡從事＿＿＿＿。）

snooker, billiard	撞球
ping-pong, table-tennis	乒乓球
badminton	羽毛球
volleyball	排球
cricket	板球
squash	壁球
tennis	網球
baseball	棒球
softball	壘球
handball	手球
hockey	曲棍球
bowling	保齡球
golf	高爾夫球
snooker	英式古典撞球
billiard	美式的花式撞球
soccer	英式足球
rugby	英式橄欖球
football	足球，美式足球
basketball	籃球

最簡單的英文自我介紹

※「打」牌，玩樂器等等，一定用 play 作為動詞。與 enjoy 連用時，改為 I enjoy playing ＿＿＿。

I play ＿＿＿.
（我玩＿＿＿。）

I play cards.
我玩撲克牌。

I enjoy playing cards.
我喜歡玩撲克牌。

chess, board game	下棋
Weiqi, the game of go	圍棋
chess	象棋
bridge	橋牌

※「從事」戶外休閒活動
以下單字使用 go ＋ Ving 或 enjoy ＋ Ving 皆可。

I go ＿＿＿ing.
（我從事＿＿＿。）

I enjoy ＿＿＿ing.
（我喜歡＿＿＿。）

scuba diving	潛水
diving	潛水，跳水
snorkeling	浮潛
surfing	衝浪

wake boarding	風浪板，水上滑板
water skiing	滑水
jet skiing	水上摩托車
parasailing	拖曳傘
catamaran sailing	雙體船
windsurfing	風帆
sailing	帆船，航行
boating	遊艇，乘船遊玩
rowing	划船
canoeing	划獨木舟
rafting	泛舟
island hopping	列島遊
cruising	巡航，出海
night fishing	夜釣
mountain climbing	爬山
camping	露營
cycling	騎腳踏車
riding	騎馬
bungee jumping	高空彈跳
biking	騎腳踏車
roller skating	滑輪
inline skating	溜直排輪
skating	滑冰
skiing	滑雪
ski board	滑雪板

★沒有嗜好

Nothing special.
我沒做什麼。

I don't have any hobby.
我沒什麼嗜好。

★特殊專長

I am adept at cooking.
我精通烹飪。

I am really good on sports field.
我在運動場上很在行。

I am good at this field.
我在這個領域很不錯。

I am very good at a lot of things.
我在很多事情上都很擅長。

I am master at digital image.
我精通數位影像。

I operate the machine very well.
我可以把機器操作得很好。

I am really good at Arts.
藝術方面我很在行。

I know the market very well.
我對市場狀況非常了解。

I am an excellent baseball player.
我是一個很出色的棒球選手。

I am excellent at communication and coordination skill.
我有優秀的溝通和協調技能。

I am familiar with PC and Microsoft Office software.
我對電腦和 Office 軟體很熟練。

＊空格中放「名詞」或「動詞 + ing」。
I am good at ＿＿＿＿＿＿.
I am very good at ＿＿＿＿＿＿.
I am master at ＿＿＿＿＿＿.
我精通於＿＿＿＿＿＿。

＊空格中放「名詞」。
I can do ＿＿＿＿＿＿ very well.
我可以把＿＿＿＿＿＿做得很好。

＊空格中放「動詞」。
I ＿＿＿＿＿＿ very well.
我＿＿＿＿＿＿很行。

＊空格中放「名詞」，通常是某一領域。
I am really good on ＿＿＿＿＿＿ field.
我在＿＿＿＿＿＿領域非常擅長。

＊空格中放「名詞」或「動詞 + ing」。
I am excellent in ＿＿＿＿＿＿.
我在＿＿＿＿＿＿領域非常優秀。

★社團

I was involved in various societies.
我參加過許多社團。

I have joined the computer club for two years
我參加過電腦社兩年的時間。

I became the volunteer of library.
我成了圖書館的志工。

I was the president of movie society.
我曾是電影社的社長。

I've never joined any society.
I've never joined any club.
我從沒加入過任何社團。

I just signed up a golf club.
我剛剛加入了高球社團。

I met a lot of people from the club.
我在社團裡認識了很多人。

I learned a lot from the club.
我在社團學了很多東西。

I was given a lot of training from the science club.
在科學研究社我獲得很多訓練。

★語言能力評鑑

I speak multiple languages.
我會說多種語言。

I am fluent in English.
我的英語流利。

I speak a little French.
我會說一點法文。

My German is very poor.
我的德語很破。

I can't read or write, but I speak pretty well.
我不懂讀和寫，但我說得很流利。

I understand Japanese.
我懂日文。

Both English and Chinese are my native language.
英語和中文都是我的母語。

I speak 3 languages, Cantonese, Chinese and English.
我會說三種語言，廣東話，中文，英文。

記憶關鍵：	
mother tongue	母語
first language	母語
second language	除母語外的第二外國語

I've passed intermediate-level GEPT.
我通過了全民英檢中級。

I have good written and oral English skills.
我有良好的英語書面和口語交流能力。

※關於語言水平，以英語為例：

English qualification	英語水平
English language proficiency	英語程度
verbal English	英語口說能力
written English	英語書寫能力
unusually outstanding	非常好
fluent	很流利
excellent	精通
distinction	表現優異
superior	優越
good	好
fair	還可以
average	一般
weak	很弱
poor	不好

※關於英語考試
TOEFL；Test of English as a Foreign Language
　　　　　　　　　　托福考試
IELTS；International English Language Testing System
　　　　　　　　　　雅思測驗
GEPT；General English Proficiency Test
　　　　　　　　　　全民英檢

· Chapter 9·

結語
Closing

★道別語

Goodbye!
I'll be seeing you.
So long!
Bye-bye!
Bye now!
Ciao!（義大利語。）
再見！

See you later!
Later!
See you around!
See ya!（See you 的簡說。）
待會兒見！

See you tomorrow.
明天見。

Take care!
Take care of yourself
保重！

Gotta go.
Got to go.
Time to leave.
Time to go.
該走了。

I'd better go now.
I have to go now.
I should leave now.
I got to be going now.
我該走了。

Let's call it a day.
今天就到此為止吧。

I am leaving.
I am about to leave.
I must leave soon.
I have to go in a few minutes.
我正要離開。
我很快就要走了。

Good day!
白天的道別語！

Good night!
晚上用的道別語！

記憶關鍵：

I am about to leave.（我正要離開。）常被人用來作為脫身
的藉口。
同一句話如果用「人名」或第三人稱「He, She」作主詞，則
可以當作下逐客令的用語。比如說，對著剛進門的另一個人
說 He is just leaving.（他正要走。）
Mr. Woody is about to leave.（Woody 先生要走了。）

★道謝

Thanks!
Thanks a lot!
A million thanks!
Thank you very much.
謝謝！

Thank you for your help.
謝謝你的幫助。

I appreciate.
I am grateful!
我很感激。

Appreciate your help.
感謝你的幫忙。

Sure!
You are welcome.
Don't mention it!
不客氣。
別客氣

My pleasure!
我的榮幸！

No big deal.
No problem.
沒問題啦！

I am glad you like it.
我很高興你喜歡！

I am glad you feel this way.
我很高興你這樣覺得！

Glad to hear that.
很高興聽到你這麼說。

★臨別時的客套語

Keep in touch!
保持聯繫！

Have a nice day!
祝你有個美好的一天！

Have a nice weekend!
週末愉快。

Have a nice trip!
Have a nice flight!
Have a pleasant trip!
Happy landing!
祝你旅途愉快！（坐飛機旅行時。）

Have a good time!
玩得愉快！

Farewell!
Bon voyage!
一路平安！

Take care!
保重！

Good luck!
祝好運！

Have Fun!
祝你玩得開心！

Thank you all for coming.
謝謝光臨。

Let's get together again.
改天再聚聚。

I had a wonderful evening!
今晚很愉快！

Hope to hear from you.
希望接到你的消息。

Nice talking to you.
很高興跟你談話。

Don't forget us.
別忘了我們喔！

It was nice meeting you.
Nice meeting you.（限用於臨別時）
It's been very pleasant to meet you.
很高興跟你會面。

Call me!
Call you!
再聯絡！（可不是真的要打電話，別誤會囉！）

Thank you for everything.
謝謝你為我所做的一切。

I hope you enjoy your stay.
我希望你在這裡時很愉快。

Please say hello to David for me.
請代我向大衛問好。

Have a nice weekend.
週末愉快！

I'd love to meet you again!
我很願意再跟你見面！

· Chapter 10 ·

簡短自我介紹
A Brief Introduction

Chapter 10
簡短自我介紹

本章依各種主題準備了幾篇簡短的自我介紹，並在旁邊加注標示，以便讀者代換成自己需要的詞彙。這樣一來，就能輕鬆完成一份獨一無二的自我介紹囉！

★商務環境自我介紹

新成員自我介紹（短篇）

這類自我介紹可長可短，視情況而定，多半是兩三句話就可以搞定。如果你希望多談些，則可以再加上「彼此共勉之」之類的客氣語。

My name is <u>Steven Chen</u>. I am the new <u>Engineer</u> of <u>RD</u> department. I am in charge of <u>memory card</u>.

姓名請改成您自己的名字。

工作類別請參照「談工作經歷～職業類別」一節修改。

in charge of　負責…
responsible for 負責
take care of　處理
工作內容請視現況修改。

中　譯：

我叫 Steven Chen。我是研發部門新來的工程師，我負責記憶卡產品。

最簡單的英文自我介紹

新成員自我介紹（稍長）

　　如果你希望多說些話，讓整篇自我介紹聽起來比較不單薄的話，再加上「很榮幸…」之類的客氣語也不錯。

My name is <u>Steven Chen</u>. I am the new <u>Engineer</u> of <u>RD</u> department, in charge of <u>memory card</u>.
It's my pleasure to become a member of this tremendous team. I can't wait to start working with you!

姓名，部門，工作執掌…等，請視現況自行修改。
比如說：
Engineer 改成 Cashier
RD 改成 Finance
這樣一來，不就成了適合財會部負責出納的新成員所使用的自我介紹了！
以下各篇範例都可以套用這個模式喔！
工作類別及部門，請參照「談工作經歷～職業類別」一節修改。

中　譯：

　　我叫 Steven Chen。我是研發部門新來的工程師，負責記憶卡。
　　能夠進入這麼棒的團隊，我感到很榮幸。我等不及要與各位共事了。

舊同仁對新同仁介紹自己

這種自我介紹多半很短，大約說一下自己的名字，最多將自己工作的部門及內容交代一下即可。

Hey! I am <u>Angela</u> with the <u>Sales</u> department.

It's great to have you with us.

> 姓名，請自行更改。

> 請置換工作的部門名稱。

歡迎對方加入團隊還有以下說法：
Welcome!（歡迎！）
Great to have you on board!（歡迎您到職。）
Great to have you in the team!
（很高興您加入我們的團隊！）
Nice to have you join us!
（很高興您加入我們的團隊！）

中　譯：

嗨！我是業務部的 Angela。很開心有你加入我們。

轉任新部門的自我介紹（轉調前後職務相似）

不同部門間轉調者，自我介紹可以從過去隸屬的部門說起。

Hello, Everyone! I am Angela, just transferred from the Headquarter. I've been working with the company for over 6 years. Glad to work with you.

姓名，請自行更改。

headquarter 總公司
branch 分公司

可以概略的說 with the company，也可以明確解釋自己原先的部門名稱。
比如說：
company 改成 sales department. 意思就變成是在業務部待過六年的意思。

也可以說：
I am looking forward to working with you.
（我很期盼和大家一同工作。）

中 譯：

　　哈囉！大家好，我是 Angela，剛剛由總公司轉調過來。我在本公司前後已經有六年囉。很高興能跟各位一同工作。

轉任新部門的自我介紹（轉調前後職務不同）

　　轉調前後的職務內容完全不同的話，可以多談些對於新職務的期盼或轉調的原因。

Hello, Everyone! I am Angela,
I've been working with the Sales
Department for almost 6 years.
It's my pleasure to transfer to the
Purchase Department.
I am a beginner as a buyer,
please be nice to me.

原來工作的部門名稱

轉調後的部門名稱

Please be nice to me.
這句話有開玩笑的成分，無論男女或職位高低都可以說。意思是：「不管過去曾有多少經驗，轉調到新職位後一切從頭開始，請大家高抬貴手啊。」

中　譯：

　　哈囉！大家好，我是 Angela，我在業務部前後已經有六年了。很高興轉調到採購部門來。當採購我是個新手，大家可要多多諒解啊！

★對新朋友自我介紹

這種自我介紹最常出現，可以用在旅行途中，對同行的新旅伴介紹自己，或是入學時對同班同學的簡短介紹也可行。尤其時下網路交友流行，更可以這樣的模式，用自身個性為重點做說明。

新同學的自我介紹

My name is Joe. I am turning 16 this Summer.
When I am free, I like to go to movies. I also enjoy playing piano very much. Baseball is my favorite sport, my friend and I usually watch live games together on the weekend.

姓名，年齡請視情況更改。

各種嗜好請參照「專長及嗜好」一節。

Live game 實況轉播的比賽。

中　譯：

我叫Joe，今年夏天就要16歲了。我有空的時候，喜歡看電影，也很喜歡彈鋼琴。另外，棒球是我最喜歡的運動，週末時我總是跟朋友一起看球賽轉播。

網友自我介紹

I am 25, single, living in Taipei.
I am fun-loving, never miss a chance to party. I am also an honest and
open hearted person. I am positive,
energetic, straight-forward and most
importantly, I have a sense of humor.

年齡，居住地點請視現況修改。

married 已婚
divorced 離婚
separated 分居中

本段針對個性上的描述，請參考「談個性秉性」一節。

中 譯：

我今年二十五歲，單身，住在台北。
我是一個風趣，喜愛社交活動的人。同時我也是一個誠實且心胸寬闊的人。我積極，有活力，並且坦率，最重要的是，我很有幽默感。

對旅遊途中認識新朋友做自我介紹

Hi, I am Joseph, just call me Joe. I come from Taiwan. It's a beautiful island.
Where are you from?

Joe 是 Joseph 的簡說，由於音節較短，容易發音，叫起來比較親切點。如果您的英文名字沒有較方便的發音，剛好也可以藉由這點，教對方唸您的名字。通常喜愛旅遊的人對異國事物也會非常感興趣的喲。

介紹完自己，當然也要聽一下對方到底是什麼來歷。所以，最後一句話以問句的方式出現，談話就很容易繼續囉！

您還可以說：

What's your name?（你叫什麼名字呢？）

When did you arrive?（你什麼時候到的？）

How long are you going to stay?（你預計待多久？）

Do you like it here?（你喜歡這裡嗎？）

Where do you plan to visit tomorrow?（明天預計要去那裡？）

I am going to the museum, too! Can I join you tomorrow?
（我也要去博物館耶！我們明天一起行動好嗎？）

中 譯：

嗨，我叫 Joseph，叫我 Joe 就好了。我來自台灣，那裡是一座美麗的小島喔。你從那裡來呢？

★履歷表封面的簡單介紹

在履歷表的封面加上一篇簡短而明確的自我介紹，可以為您的履歷加分喔！

有工作經驗者

有過工作經驗的人，除了可以提到自己的學歷出身以外，也建議強調自己曾完成過的事蹟。

Greetings! I was a <u>full-time</u> <u>system analyst</u> for the past 3 years. <u>I had implemented ERP software.</u> This experience had enhanced my abilities to handle multiple assignments <u>under stress.</u>
I would like to combine my experience with my ability to become an enthusiastic team player who will make a positive contribution to the company.

part-time 兼職
full-time 全職

請改為您過去曾擔任的職位及經驗年限。

描述過去工作成效。

work under pressure
= work under stress
在壓力下工作

中 譯：

大家好！我曾是一位全職的系統分析師，有三年的經驗，完成過 ERP 軟體的上線工程。這項經驗使我在壓力下有同時處理多項事務的能力。我的目標是能夠結合現有的經驗及能力，以熱忱的工作態度，為團隊創造利益。

最簡單的英文自我介紹

沒有工作經驗者

沒有工作經驗的人，重點則要放在展現自己積極的個性及學習速度快等優點。

Greetings! I just received a <u>Master's degree</u> in <u>Computer Science</u>. I don't have any experience, but <u>I learn things quickly</u> and I love <u>challenges</u>. Hope to hear from you soon.

---

graduate degree 學士學位
master degree 碩士學位
= second degree
= postgraduate degree
Ph.D degree 博士學位
請參照「談學習經歷」一節。

I am an enthusiastic learner.
（我熱愛學習。）
請參考「談個性秉性」一節，代換成說明自己個性的形容詞。

中 譯：

大家好！我剛剛獲得電腦科學碩士學位。我沒有任何經驗，但是我學習速度快且喜愛面對挑戰。
希望能盡快聽到您的回音。

應徵自由接案的工作

　　自由接案者沒有工作地點的限制，只要按時完成工作，交出成績就可以囉！

I am a freelance <u>programmer</u> looking for a <u>long term</u> contract. My name is <u>John</u>, I am in <u>Taoyuan</u>.

工作類別請參照「談工作經歷」一節填入。

long term　長期
short term　短期
temp. = temporary
臨時工，短期工。

姓名及居住地，記得依情況做修改。

中　譯：

　　我是一個自由接案的程式設計師，我希望能找到一個長期合作的案子。我的名字叫做 John，住在桃園。

應徵一般工作都可以用的簡短介紹

I am a <u>nanny</u> with <u>5 years</u> experience and great references. I am <u>patient</u>, I love working <u>with babies and toddlers</u>. I also have obtained a <u>nanny</u> qualifications.

Prior to being a <u>nanny</u>, I was working as a nurse in <u>Pediatrics</u> for almost <u>6 years</u>.

I am looking forward to working for you.

工作類別，及經驗長短，請自行依現況修改。

patient 可用適當的形容詞代換，請參考「談個性秉性」一節。

可以改為：
-work with people 跟人合作，強調自己喜歡與人相處的特質。
-work along 獨自工作，表示自己可以獨當一面，完成任務的特質。

過去經驗及工作性質，請依自己的情況做調整。請參照「談工作經歷」一節。

中　譯：

　　我是一名擁有五年經驗的褓母，同時我有很好的介紹人資訊供您查詢。我很有耐心，喜歡與幼兒相處。並且擁有合格保母證書。在成為保母之前，我曾在醫院小兒科擔任過護士工作六年。期盼能為您工作。

以所應徵的工作為主題做簡單的自我介紹

I am a Taiwanese. I just finished my first degree in Taipei University, major in Education.
I also have obtained the Certificate in Child Care and Education. I am looking for an opportunity to become a teacher. I am sure that I am the right person you are looking for.
I can start to work in early July. Hope to hear from you soon.

國籍請參照「談基本資料」一節修改。

學籍資料也起請參照「談學習經歷」一節修改。

曾經獲得過的證照名稱一定要寫對喔！

工作類別請參照「談工作經歷～職業類別」一節修改。

early	早期，月初
beginning	早期，月初
mid	中期
end	晚期，月底
late	晚期，月底

Jan.	一月	Feb.	二月	Mar.	三月	Apr.	四月
May	五月	Jun.	六月	Jul.	七月	Aug.	八月
Sep.	九月	Oct.	十月	Nov.	十一月	Dec.	十二月

中 譯：

我是台灣人，剛剛自台北大學獲得學士學位，主修教育。同時我也擁有幼教合格證書。我希望能夠成為一位老師，並且我確信自己就是您們需要的人。我大約七月初可以開始工作，希望很快可以收到您們的回應。

·Chapter 11·

一分鐘寫自傳
Biography

★ 自傳的基本架構

　　前面章節談過了較簡短的口語式自我介紹，很簡單吧！希望讀者們都能自由運用各種情境，發展成屬於自己的一篇簡介。接下來，本章就練習一下，如何把前面介紹過的句子，湊成一整篇完整的自傳吧！

　　自傳的架構不脫五大主題：

一、　描述基本資料和家庭背景

二、　描述自己的個性

三、　描述自己的嗜好或專長

四、　針對主題做延伸，比如說：

　　　─應徵工作時：談談自己所具備的條件，以及適合該職位的理由。

　　　─申請學校時：談談選擇該校或該系的原因。

　　　─參加活動時：談談參與該活動的感想或原因，譬如：為什麼想參加座談會，上次參與活動的感想…等。

　　　─談生平經歷：描述過去曾經歷過的事件如何影響自己的人生，並談談感想。

五、　結束語

最簡單的英文自我介紹

工作自傳範例：

記得喔！請參考本書前面的章節，將畫底線的內容換成適用於您自己的詞語。很快的，您的自傳就完成囉！

My name is <u>Joe</u>, I was born on <u>Sep 21, 1988</u> in <u>Taipei</u>. I grow up in a great family of <u>three</u> members. <u>I am the only child</u>. My father is a <u>businessman</u> who works in a <u>local company</u>. My mother is a <u>housewife</u>, she is the most <u>caring and tender</u> person in the world. This is where I grow up, ordinary, simple and full of happiness. I am an <u>easygoing</u> person with <u>optimistic</u> character. I love <u>movies</u> and <u>musics</u>. I <u>exercise</u> regularly, too. My favorite recreational activity is <u>traveling</u>. <u>If I have a vacation, I will plan a trip to Egypt.</u>	姓名，居住地，出生日期等請改成您自己的資訊。
	-I have 2 brothers. （我有兩個兄弟。） -I have a younger sister. （我有一個妹妹。） -younger　較年少的 -elder sister　較年長的
	請參照「談基本資料」一節，概略描述父母的職業
	為使文章看來豐富，請參照「談個性秉性」一節，概略描述父母的個性。
	請同樣參照「談個性秉性」一節，描述自己的性格，由於這篇自傳談的對象是您自己，所以，跟自己有關的描述，可不能太隨便喔！
	請參照「專長及嗜好」一節，描述自己的的嗜好！
	這句話只是自傳的主人下一個想要旅遊的目的地。當然，您可以把這句話省略，也可以改為： I will plan a trip to any corner of the world. （我可能會計劃到世界上任何一個角落去旅行。）

When I started working as a sales in DSC Co., it was just a small office. I was trained to work along. I also make sure every process was executed completely. Undoubtedly, it was a great training for a fresh graduate. I was able to accomplish tasks by utlizing limited resources. The most importantly, I gained many experiences from the independent working style.

After 3 years, I decided to leave this company, I would like to become a sales of IC disign industry. This is a relatively new market which excites me a lot. I feel that this would allow me to learn more skills. I love challenges and I look forward to working with others as a team.

Sales 請依照「談工作經歷」一節修改。
DSC Co. 及 just a small office，也請依照您的實際狀況修正喔。

fresh graduate 就是我們常說的社會新鮮人。改為：
It was a great training for me.（這對我而言是一項很棒的訓練。）
就適用於任何人囉。

在前公司的工作經驗年數，請自行做修改。

Sales 是將來希望做的職位，請依您的目標修改喔！請參照「談工作經歷」一節。
IC disign industry 是將來希望進入的產業，也可以改成所應徵公司的名稱，強調你進入這家公司的決心。

針對您想要應徵這個職位的理由，或您所具備的條件發表看法。以積極、有計畫性的字眼來表達，比較容易獲得青睞喔！

I am thrilled by the <u>new mar-ket</u>. Sincerely hope that I would have this opportunity to work for your company.

請以新職位之所以吸引您的條件代入或是：
I am thrilled by the new opportunity.
（我對新的機會感到非常興奮）

中　譯：

　　我叫Joe，1988年9月21日出生於台北。我生長在一個很棒的家庭，一共有三位成員，我是家裡的獨生子。我父親在一家台商公司工作，是一個生意人。我母親是家庭主婦，說她是世界上最慈愛的人也不為過。我就是在這樣一個平凡、簡單而充滿幸福的家庭長大的。

　　我的個性隨和樂觀，我喜歡看電影，聽音樂，有固定運動的習慣。我最喜歡的休閒活動是旅行，只要有長一點的假期，我可能會計劃到埃及去玩。

　　我一開始在DSC公司擔任業務工作時，那裡是一間小公司。在那裡，我必須獨自完成所有工作，確認每一項流程都獲得完整的執行。毫無疑問地，對於一位剛畢業的社會新鮮人而言，這是最好的訓練。我學到了如何利用有限的資源完成被指派的任務。最重要的，在這種獨立工作的模式下，我獲得許多寶貴的經驗。

　　三年後，我決定離開這家公司，我希望能進入 IC disign 產業成為業務。這是一個相當新的市場，新的事物總是令我精神一振，我想這個新經驗一定能帶領我學習到更多的技能。我喜愛接受挑戰，更期盼能夠成為團隊合作中的一員。

　　對於新市場我感到非常興奮，誠摯希望能夠有機會為貴公司效力。

求學自傳範例：

My name is <u>Simon</u>, I was born on <u>Oct 25, 1989</u> in <u>Tainan</u>. I grow up in a great family of <u>five</u> members. My father is a <u>farme</u>, my mother is <u>his best assistant</u>. They work in a <u>fruit farm</u>. My sisters and I used to help them after school.

I am a <u>quiet</u> person. My favorit amusement is <u>reading</u> and <u>listening to musics</u>. I enjoy <u>musicals</u> and <u>operas</u> as well. When I come across setbacks, anything involves <u>melody</u> would cheer me up.

I took a <u>dual major</u> in <u>international trades</u> and <u>French</u> as my <u>undergraduate degree</u>. <u>After two years working as a journalist,</u> I think it's a good choice for me to apply for a <u>Master's degree</u> in <u>Political Science</u>. I've made up my mind to become a specialist in this field. Hope a professional training in <u>Central University</u> will reinforce my faith in this goal.

指第一段

發現了嗎？第一段的基本資料跟前一篇範例其實差不多，僅僅將基本資料改換一下，句子對調一番就完成囉！

指第二段

第二段描述自己的個性，同樣的將重點字改換成適當的文字，就輕鬆完成囉！
amusement 消遣，娛樂與第一段中的 recreation 同義。
cheer sb up 振奮某人的精神。

請參考「談學習經歷」一節，將過去的主修科目及學歷換成適用自己的詞語。

過去的工作經驗請參考「談工作經歷」一節置換。
如果沒有工作經驗則可以省略這句話。

請參考「談學習經歷」一節，將欲申請的主修科目及學歷換成正確的詞語。

請改寫為欲申請之學校名稱。

最簡單的英文自我介紹

<u>Department of Political Science</u> in <u>Central</u> University is my only choice. I hope I could have the chance to become a student here. Sincerely awaiting good news from you.

請改寫為欲申請之學校名稱及系名。

中　譯：

　　我叫 Simon，1989 年 10 月 25 日出生於台南。我生長在一個五口之家。我的父親是一位農夫，母親則是父親最好的幫手。他們在果園裏工作，我和姐妹們經常在放學後到果園裏面幫忙。

　　我的性格溫和，最喜歡的娛樂是閱讀及聽音樂。對於音樂劇或歌劇也非常喜愛。每當我感到低潮，任何有旋律的東西都能令我精神一振。

　　我的學士學位是國際貿易及法文雙主修，在兩年的記者工作經驗之後，我想申請政治學碩士是一個不錯的選擇。我已下定決心要在這個領域成為一位專家，希望 Central 大學所提供的專業訓練能更加實踐這項理想。

　　Central 大學的政治學系是我唯一的選擇，希望有機會能夠成為這所大學的學生。誠摯地等候您的好消息。

★自傳常用單字分類

工作成就相關

accomplish	完成，成就
implement	完成，實施
achievement	工作成就，業績
break the record	打破記錄
execute	實行，實施
perform	執行，履行
valuable	有價值的
top	最高的，最好的
succeed	成功
plan	計畫
target	目標，指標
overcome	克服
behave	表現
demonstrate	證明，示範
enlarge	擴大
participate in	參加
adapted to	適應於
project	專案
representative	代表，代理人
perfect	使改善，完美
motivate	促進，激發
effect	效果，作用

最簡單的英文自我介紹

實驗設計發明相關

design	設計
develop	開發，發揮
devise	設計，發明
survey	調查
research	調查，研究
reinforce	加強，增援
originate	創始，發明
regenerate	刷新，重建
renew	重建，換新
install	安裝
introduce	採用，引進
refine	精練，精製，提煉
generate	產生
inspired	受啟發的，受鼓舞的
enrich	使豐富
evaluation	估價，評價
study	研究
test	試驗，檢驗
rehash	重新處理
rehandle	重新處理
integrate	使結合，使一體化
invent	發明

工程製造採購相關

maintain	保持，維修
repair	修復，修補
make	製造
promote	生產，製造
manufacture	製造
standard	標準，規格
operate	操作(機器等)
supply	供給
demand	需求
monitor	監督
verify	證實，證明
provide	提供，供應
material	材料，原料

資源運用相關

useful	有用的
use	使用，運用
utilize	利用
replace	接替，替換
receive	得到，接受，收到
unify	使統一
work	工作
vivify	使活躍

敘述業績／數字相關

negotiate	談判
exploit	功勳，功績
create	創造
double	加倍，翻一倍
redouble	加倍，倍增
level	水準
increase	增加
reduce	減少，降低
decrease	減少
lessen	減少
spread	擴大
profit	利潤
cost	成本，費用
earn	賺取，獲得
analyze	分析
worth	使…有價值
total	總數，總額
reach	達到
revenue	營業額
raise	提高
realize	了解，實現
goal	目標

target	目標
market	市場，行銷
promote	促銷
show	表明，顯示
recover	恢復，彌補
consolidate	合併，匯總
reconsolidate	重新鞏固，重新整頓
shorten	減低，縮短
lengthen	延長

輔助協辦相關

type	打字
sponsor	主辦
strengthen	加強，鞏固
translate	翻譯
recorded	記載的

問題解決相關

solve	解決
settle	解決
complaint	抱怨
claim	抱怨
resolve	解決
sort out	清理

管理控制相關

direct	指導
eliminate	消除
manage	管理，經營
renovate	革新，修理
innovate	改革，革新
reform	改革
reconstruct	重建
rectify	整頓
lead	領導
guide	指導，操縱
streamline	使有效率，使合理化
systematize	使系統化
regularize	使系統化
modernize	使現代化
simplify	簡化，精簡
supervise	監督，管理
recognize	認清，辨識
influence	影響
control	控制
significant	意義重大的，影響重大的
conduct	經營，處理
improve	改進，提高

regulate	控制，管理
expedite	加快，促進
speed up	加速
set record	創紀錄
localize	使地方化
authorized	委任的，核准的
break through	驚人的進展，關鍵問題的解決

· Chapter 12 ·

談話的藝術
The Art of
Conversation

★不該談的話題□

到底哪些話題是「非問品」呢？如果是很熟的朋友，當然百無禁忌，什麼都可以談。但各國國情不同，在初次見面的社交場合裡，如何聊得盡興又能兼顧應有的禮貌呢？

或許這些話題其實沒那麼嚴重，但在不了解對方的狀況下，多注意一點畢竟不會錯的。針對禁忌話題（taboo），就讓我們為您做個整理吧！

在公開場合請盡量避免以下的敏感話題（Sensitive Topics）：

✗有政治傾向的話題

✗婚姻或感情狀況

✗薪資或財產

✗年齡隱私

✗身體缺陷

✗評論身材，尤其是針對女性

✗女性在場時不要過於著墨軍中經歷…等男性話題

✗有色話題不要聊，尤其是女性在場時

✗私密問題，如性傾向…等問題

✗不要一直重複同樣的話題

✗敏感的商業問題

✗不要用自己的方言（dialect）交談

✗不要說髒話，要用優雅的辭彙

✗盡量避免直接問任何關於對方的問題，改以誘導的方式使對方說出自己的看法。

最簡單的英文自我介紹

私人問題少聊

What's your weight?
你體重多少？

How tall are you?
你身高多少？

Do you have a boyfriend / girlfriend?
你有男朋友/女朋友嗎？

Are you married?
你結婚了嗎？

　　不能問私人問題其實沒有什麼特別的原因，多半是顧及個人心理的感覺。試想，如果你一直希望自己身型能夠豐滿一點或是纖瘦一點，或是你一直想找個伴侶但卻總碰不到合意的交往對象，是否會很在意這類的問題呢？所以囉，在社交場合上交談，這樣的問題若問錯了對象，可是很尷尬的，還是少聊為妙吧！

政治宗教話題別碰

Which party do you support?
你支持哪一個政黨？

What is your religion?
你信什麼教？

　　如果大家的政治及宗教信仰方向一致，的確可以激發出驚人的團結力量，創造人心和諧。然而，當雙方的信仰有些抵觸的話，卻也可能造成不必要的爭端。所以這樣的話題，別多談也許是個好建議喔。

膚色種族話題要小心

　　與政治話題一樣，膚色或種族也是價值觀及主觀的信仰。也因為民情不同，對語言不熟悉，一不小心就很容易造成對方不舒服的感受。為避免造成說者無意，聽者卻有心的遺憾。

　　比如說，形容東方人時 oriental（東方的）這個字帶有一點貶抑的味道，以 Asian（亞裔）來替代比較好。比如說：

She is an oriental woman.（她是一位東方女性。）
She is an Asian woman.（她是一位亞裔女性。）

其他不適當的字還有：

不適當字眼	適當字眼
Nigger（黑鬼）	Black（黑人）
Chink（清客，中國佬）	Chinese（中國人）
Japs（日本佬）	Japanese（日本人）
Heinies（德國佬）	German（德國人）
Kraut（德國佬）	German（德國人）
Frogs（法國佬）	Frenchmen（法國人）
Wops（義大利佬）	Italian（義大利人）
Guinea（義大利佬）	Italian（義大利人）
Limey（英國佬）	English（英國人）
Spic（西班牙佬）	Spanish（西班牙人）

與性有關的話題別談

與性有關的話題，最直接的就是黃色笑話。為什麼黃色笑話別亂說，這就不用再多做解釋了吧！面對異性，不當的性話題可能令對方產生聯想，以為你有特別的企圖，這樣一來可就麻煩囉。

另外，與性向有關的話題，同樣沒有必要在公共場合談論。無論如何，人家喜歡的對象是同性還是異性，沒有必要向你交待吧。

與性話題相關的詞語有：

sexual subject	性話題
sexual orientation	性傾向
dirty joke	黃色笑話
lesbian	女同性戀
gay	男同性戀
straight	異性戀
heterosexual	異性戀
homosexual	同性戀
sexual harassment	性騷擾

年齡不要問

How old are you?
你幾歲？

尤其問女性年齡，是很不禮貌的一件事。大部分的女性很在意自己的外貌，而年輕多半也是美麗的條件之一。所以囉，女性的年齡也因此變成了一個敏感話題。

收入不能問

What is your income?
How much money do you make?
你的收入是多少？

收入問題很敏感，尤其是男性朋友的收入也是非問品之一。為避免讓對方有不舒服的感覺，還是先別問吧。

與錢有關的問題少聊些

How much did you pay for your dress?
這件衣服你花多少錢買的？

不管買貴了或是買便宜了，這個答案一說出來，都會有些尷尬，所以別聊這個了。

★絕對安全的話題

　　那麼多東西不該聊，那麼到底能聊什麼呢？真的不知道該談什麼的話，就談天氣吧！外國人談天氣幾乎跟中國人隨時都能以「吃飽沒？」打招呼一樣平常。除此之外，本章還提供你一些好主意喔！

談天氣準沒錯

How is the weather out there?
外面的天氣如何?

Is it going to rain tomorrow?
明天會下雨嗎?

Lovely weather, isn't it?
It's sunny, isn't it?
天氣真好，是吧?

It's burning up out there.
天氣好熱。

It's turning out cloudy.
天氣開始轉陰了。

You are soaked!
你溼透了!

<u>其他與天氣相關的詞語還有：</u>

fine, fair, sunny, clear	晴朗
mild, warm	溫暖
cool	涼爽
hot	炎熱
cloudy	多雲
overcast, dull, gloomy	陰天
drizzle	毛毛雨，小雨
shower	陣雨
thunder shower	雷陣雨
pour, downpour	大雨
storm	暴風雨
thunder storm	雷雨
seasonal rain	季節雨
monsoon	季風，雨季
sleet	雨夾雪
thunder	打雷
lightning	閃電
snowy	有雪
light snow	小雪
blizzard	暴風雪
snowstorm	暴風雪
hail, hailstone	冰雹

avalanche	雪崩
ice storm	冰雹
windy	有風
breezy	微風陣陣
gale	大風
windy and dusty	風沙
gust	強陣風
foggy	有霧
frosty	霜凍
chilly	微冷
freezing	冰冷
misty	薄霧
dry	乾燥的
damp, humid	潮濕的，有濕氣的
stuffy	不通風的，悶熱的
dust storm	沙塵暴
tsunami	海嘯
typhoon	颱風
hurricane	颶風
tornado, twister	龍捲風
flood	洪水
drought	旱災
earthquake	地震
landslide	山崩

mudslide	土石流
volcanic eruption	火山爆發
natural disaster	天然災害
calamity	災難
disaster-hit area	災區
death tolls	死亡人數，死亡率
casualty	遇難者，傷亡人員
hot wave	熱浪
global warming	全球暖化
greenhouse effect	溫室效應
El Nino	聖嬰現象
carbon dioxide	二氧化碳
emit	排放
global temperature	全球溫度
rise	上升

談文化差異最有趣

Where are you from?
你從哪裡來？

How do you say "How are you" in your language?
用你的語言怎麼說「你好嗎」？

Do you enjoy your stay here?
Do you like it here?
你喜歡這裡嗎？

How long will you stay?
你會在這裡多久？

Do you like our food?
你喜歡吃我們的食物嗎？

What is it like in China?
中國怎麼樣？

How's your vacation?
你假期過得如何啊？

其餘例句請參考本書「談基本資料」，居住環境一節，這裡不再重複。

以剛剛發生的事情為主軸

Great movie, isn't?
電影滿好看的，你覺得呢？（在電影發表會上）

Nice dissert, right?
甜點還不錯，對吧？（茶會或聚餐場合）

Isn't it nice?
真是不錯吧？

This is a nice game.
This is a good match.
這是一場很精采的比賽。

以共同話題開啟談話

I am in the movie society, too.
我也是電影社的成員。

I am in the fraternity.
我參加兄弟會。

I am in the sorority.
我參加姊妹會。

最簡單的英文自我介紹

★個人資料表重點資訊（中英對照）

CV; curriculum vitae	簡歷
personal details	個人資料
photo	照片
Chinese name	中文姓名
English name	英文姓名
first name	名
given name	名字
middle name	中名
maiden name	女人在結婚前的姓
last name	姓
surname	姓
family name	姓氏
marriage status	婚姻狀況
marital status	婚姻狀況
single	未婚
married	已婚
citizenship	國籍
nationality	國籍
country of citizenship	國籍，出生地
country of birth	國籍
nationality	國籍
native language	母語

sex	性別
gender	性別
M; male	男性
F; female	女性
date of birth	出生日期
birth date	出生日期
Y; year	年份
M; month	月份
D; date	日期
dd/mm/yyyy	日／月／年
I.D. No.	身份證號碼
contact info.	聯絡資訊
address	地址
permanent address	永久住址
telephone	電話
fax	傳真
area code	區碼
E-mail	電子郵件
present occupation	職業
race or ethnicity	種族
White, non-Hispanic	白人，非西班牙人
Black, non-Hispanic	黑人，非西班牙人
Caucasian	白種人
Hispanic	西班牙人

Latino	拉美洲人
Asian	亞洲人
Pacific Islander	太平洋群島人士
American Indian	印第安人
Native Alaskan	阿拉斯加原住民
physically disabled	肢殘人士
learning disabled	學習障礙人士
chronic diseases	慢性病
contact person	聯絡人
emergency contact	緊急聯絡人
relationship	關係
education history	教育背景
educational background	教育背景
academic history	學歷
level	程度
level of study completed	最高學歷
graduate level education	研究所學歷
undergraduate level education	大學學歷
high school	中學畢業
vocational school	職業學校
secondary education	中學
university	大學
college	大學
others	其它學歷

name of school	畢業學校名稱
address of school	畢業學校地址
name of institution	校名
major	主修
period of enrollment	修業年限
years of study	修業年限
diploma or degree	文憑或學位
secondary education status	次高學歷狀況
home schooled	在家自學
professional experience	工作經歷
work experience	工作經歷
position	職位
type of work	工作性質
employer	雇主
degree received	已取得的學位
degree earned	已取得的學位
English qualification	英語水平
English language proficiency	英語程度
verbal English	英語口說能力
written English	英語書寫能力
unusually outstanding	非常好
fluent	很流利
excellent	精通
distinction	表現優異

superior	優越
good	好
fair	還可以
average	一般
weak	很弱
poor	不好
recommendation for admission	入學用推薦信
appraiser	推薦者
confidential	機密
referee	推薦人
reference	推薦信
recommendation	推薦信
capacity	關係，用在推薦信中，如：capacity as his professor

國家圖書館出版品預行編目資料

最簡單的英文自我介紹／陳久娟編著.
　--初版.--臺北縣汐止市： 雅典文化, 民96.12
　　面；公分. -- 英語工具書系列：04）
　　ISBN：978-986-7041-49-4
　1.英語　　2.會話

805.188　　　　　　　　　　　　　96020539

最簡單的英文自我介紹

編　　著◎陳久娟
出 版 者◎雅典文化事業有限公司
登 記 證◎局版北市業字第五七〇號
發 行 人◎黃玉雲
執行編輯◎陳久娟
編 輯 部◎221 台北縣汐止市大同路三段 194-1 號 9 樓
　　　　　EmailAdd: a8823.a1899@msa.hinet.net
　　　　　電話◎02-86473663　傳真◎ 02-86473660
郵　　撥◎18965580 雅典文化事業有限公司
法律顧問◎永信法律事務所　林永頌律師
總 經 銷◎永續圖書有限公司
　　　　　221 台北縣汐止市大同路三段 194-1 號 9 樓
　　　　　EmailAdd: yungjiuh@ms45.hinet.net
　　　　　網站◎ www.foreverbooks.com.tw
　　　　　郵撥◎ 18669219
　　　　　電話◎ 02-86473663　傳真◎ 02-86473660
初　　版◎2007 年 12 月
定　　價◎ NT$ 250 元